THIS BOOK IS NOT YET RATED

A NOVEL BY

PETER BOGNANNI

 DIAL BOOKS

DIAL BOOKS

An imprint of Penguin Random House LLC · New York

Copyright © 2019 by Peter Bognanni.

Visit us online at penguinrandomhouse.com

CIP Data is available.

Printed in the United States of America

ISBN 9780735228078

1 3 5 7 9 10 8 6 4 2

Text set in Neutraface · Designed by Jason Henry

For Sal Bognanni

ETHAN'S GLOSSARY OF FILM TERMS
ENTRY #1

FADE IN:

A completely black screen. Then, slowly,
an image becomes visible.

You've seen it a thousand times. First
darkness. Then the light.

Sound next. A face maybe. A landscape.

A world born before your eyes. One minute
you're sitting there in the dim theater with
a room full of strangers, and the next you
are somewhere else.

It only takes a second, but it feels like
magic every time.

A Fade In says: Welcome.

It says: *Shhhhhh*

A story is about to start.

1

When I was fourteen, I started watching a movie a day.

No exceptions.

It wasn't always easy to fit them in.

There was life to contend with. Homework. Job. School. Sustenance. The occasional human interaction. But I tried my best to do it no matter what. No matter how tired I might be. Saturdays were my binge days when I left reality behind for hours, cocooned in my vintage Star Wars bedspread with only a box of cereal and a warm Dr Pepper to get me through the day. Sundays I rested, like the Lord.

Then I watched a movie.

I'm seventeen now, so if you do the math, that's three years at 365 days a year. Which is 1,095 total days. With an average run time of about 90 minutes a movie, that's at least 1,642 hours. Or, if you prefer: 68 days.

Sixty-eight days of movie time. Sixty-eight days of being someone else.

For a person who spends most of his life indoors, I've done some fairly epic things during those hours. For example: I've stormed a castle with some samurai in feudal Japan, which I totally recommend. I've done heroin in Scotland and watched a zombie baby crawl on the ceiling (don't recommend). I've been a piano prodigy, a submarine captain, and a prison inmate, not necessarily in that order. I have whispered my secrets into a tree, pulled a human heart from a toilet, and walked a tightrope across the New York skyline in a pair of revealing tights.

And whenever my mother or anyone else well-meaning asks me why I spend so much time in a darkened room, staring at a glowing screen, I answer with a question of my own: Why do you live one life? As in: Why be content with one life when you could live one thousand and ninety-five? A few of them are bound to be more interesting than your own. Or in my case: most of them.

Aside from a few movies by this Japanese director, Ozu, and long sections of *The Hobbit*, which should have been called *The Desolation of My Attention Span*, it doesn't take much to beat the movie of my life these days.

For one thing, I work at a dying movie theater. That should come as no surprise. The movie part, anyway. It pays almost nothing, but it makes my daily quota a little easier to meet. Though I should clarify right off the bat that by "work at," I mean *am the boss of.* I used to be just another humble employee of the Green Street Cinema in Minneapolis, Minnesota, but then the owner, Randy, had a personal crisis, skipped town, and left me in charge during his absence. He never came back.

I have two theories about why he chose me.

The first is that I am the longest-standing employee of the Green Street aside from Sweet Lou, our organ player, who is maybe two hundred years old.

And second: Randy was once pretty chummy with my dad, who used to be the chair of the Film Studies Department at the university down the street. For these reasons, I am currently the captain of this sinking ship.

Ahoy there, movie nerds. All aboard.

Call me Wendy.

That's not my name. My name is Ethan, but Wendy is what everyone here calls me since I became de facto manager. If you haven't guessed already—and why would you?— it's a Peter Pan reference, and not a very clever one at that. I'm not sure how it got started, but one day I came in with the new schedules for the week and everyone was saying it with the same smirk on their faces.

I guess that makes my crew of barely employable movie geeks the Lost Boys. They aren't all boys, but they are definitely lost anywhere other than this theater.

So Wendy it is.

I've learned to live with it. Just like I've learned to live with the smell of curdled butter, the perpetually clogged toilet in the employee bathroom, and the fact that I never see the projectionist leave the premises. But before I get too caught up in the details, I should let you know why any of this matters.

It all got started on a day when I thought my only problem was going to be the rats.

Rats, you say?

We had many. They enjoyed eating candy. Specifically the candy we stored to serve at our concession stand. But this was the first day a rat-chewed candy box had been served to a customer. Which is how my only break of the day was disturbed.

I was standing outside the theater, when Griffin, the stoned ticket taker, walked up behind me and cleared his throat.

"Um. Wendy?" he said.

I knew Griffin was stoned because Griffin is always stoned. If he came to work sober, planets would drift out of alignment. The tides would reverse. Or . . . he might just do his job competently. His favorite director is Terry Gilliam, and at last count, he had seen *Fear and Loathing in*

Las Vegas fifty-four times. He tried to re-enact it once, but he didn't have a car, and he only made it to the city limits on his ten-speed before he got distracted by the extensive beef jerky selection at SuperAmerica.

"Remember what I said about bothering me on break?" I asked Griffin.

Griffin scratched the back of his neck. He pushed his enormous black glasses up his nose. His mop of dark hair obscured the top third of the lenses.

"You said not to do it."

"That is correct," I said.

Longest pause ever.

"The rats ate most of the Dots," he said.

"I know," I said. "I saw the mess this morning."

"Right," he said. "So, I gave a lady a box that I thought was fine, but turned out to be kinda *compromised*, rat-wise, and she left saying she was going to sue all of us. Like personally. Everyone who works here."

"Uh-huh," I said.

"Well," he said, "I've been thinking it over, and I'm just not sure my finances can take that kind of hit right now."

I took a glance at the cloudless sky above me. There was an airplane inching its way through the blue, leaving a breathy white trail behind it. I imagined myself in an aisle seat, sipping a ginger ale and laughing at a movie I would never pay to watch. I had about five seconds to enjoy this fantasy before I walked to the entrance of the Green Street, shoved open the glass doors, and smelled the stale popcorn and musty carpeting.

"Yo, Wendy!" said Lucas, an international student from the U who worked concessions. "The rats got into the candy again! Your traps aren't working, my man."

I passed him without comment, trying to remember if he'd ever actually been hired, or if he'd just walked behind the counter one day in his Bill Murray T-shirt and never left. His mom was American, but he grew up with his dad in Lebanon, watching pirated tapes from the States. He had seen more movies than any of us combined, and he rarely let us forget it.

"He knows, dude," said Griffin, "And he knows about the lawsuit. Wendy has a lot on his mind right now."

I left them behind to discuss my mind. Meanwhile, I walked down the main hallway to the storage room where there was probably some kind of massive rat orgy taking place at that very moment. I did this because, even though I am underage and technically too young to be a manager, I am somehow a manager. And even though I haven't been able to "manage" many things in my own life, I still felt like trying at the Green Street. It was maybe the last place I felt like trying.

Because, if I'm honest, things had been a little rough of recent.

And by "of recent," I mean the three years since my dad died.

He died just before I turned fourteen, and it's still hard for me to say it or even write about it without getting depressed and angry and then depressed again. For now I'll just say: It was quick and surprising. And afterward, I kind of took a hall pass from life. My grades went south. Things with my mom got weird. And to make matters worse, my best friend moved away. In the years that followed, I kinda stopped thinking about college. And basically the only thing I didn't give up on entirely was watching movies and doing my job at the Green Street. Which, come to think of it, is probably why Randy made me temporary manager.

That and someone had to deal with the rats.

I opened the door now to the storage room and things were eerily quiet. If my life were a movie, there would have been some slightly out-of-tune violins starting in the background. Maybe a close-up of a single bead of sweat on my forehead. Inside the closet there were boxes of candy that had been knocked from the shelves. Raisinets. Twizzlers. Mike and Ikes. An all-you-can-eat buffet.

On top of the pile was a single rat the size of a small raccoon. I only slightly exaggerate his size. He was the rodent king of candy hill. Lord of the Junior Mints. Master of Milk Dud Mountain. His two bottom teeth looked sharpened to kill, and I'm pretty sure he was in a diabetic coma.

"Begone, Brando!" I said.

I had decided to name him Brando (after late career Marlon Brando).

No reaction. I looked at the traps I bought last week: Empty.

I picked up a nearby broom, and I was about to take a swing at him when I received another tap on the shoulder. Which caused me to jump and scream louder and higher than I have ever screamed maybe in my life. Griffin dropped his glasses.

"Whoa," he said. "Sorry, man."

"Jesus, Griffin!" I yelled when I turned around. "I thought you were a rat."

He stared at me wide-eyed. He seemed a little frightened at this possibility.

"I'm not," he said.

I looked over at Brando, but he was long gone.

"What are you doing here?" I asked. "What could possibly be so important that you need to interrupt me in the middle of an attempted murder?"

Griffin took his signature pause, reaching down to pick up his glasses.

"There's a man here with some papers. He says we're being evicted."

2

O nce upon a time, when I was younger, Dad and I used to go to the movies.

Like once a week at least when my mom worked Saturdays. It was our day, and we had a ritual. We always got to the theater early enough to see all the previews. We always got one big popcorn to share and two individual boxes of Nerds (our mascot). We always went to the bathroom right before the movie to avoid mid-film emergencies. And when we got inside the theater, we connected straws together so that they could go from the sodas on the floor all the way up to our mouths—that way we would never have to look away. Afterward, we each had to answer two questions.

1) What was the image from the film that we just couldn't shake?

And:

2) How was the last line?

And the Green Street Cinema is where we went the most. Dad didn't like the multiplexes. He thought they were soulless and bland. Besides, the Green Street was right down the street from the university where he taught, and everyone knew him there. The concession guys gave him extra butter. And most Saturdays I got in free. "If that kid can sit through *Das Boot*," the cashier once said, "it's on the house." I started volunteering there before I was old enough to work, and even before that, I hung around while Dad did his college film screenings.

I would watch him from the back row as he gesticulated in front of the screen, saying outrageous things in his lecture about *Rear Window*, like, "Clearly Hitchcock is taking on impotence here! Right? Look at that phallic cast on Jefferies! But he can't *do* anything!" and ignoring the chuckles that followed. His hair was curly and he didn't get it cut often enough. Mom used to say he looked like the professor from central casting, but it wasn't quite that bad. He was surprisingly athletic. He played pickup basketball, and once when I went to the college gym, I saw him sink a jump hook from the free-throw line over the outstretched arm of a winded biology professor. It was a thing of beauty.

But still, he never seemed more at home than at the Green Street. It was his home away from home, and especially after he died, it became mine, too. These days I usually came in at eight a.m. only to leave at six or seven that night after every smooshed Milk Dud had been scraped from the floor. I still changed each letter on the antique marquee by hand. And I could feel it in my soul when a spring popped loose on our duct-taped seats.

Which is why my heart nearly stopped when I first held the papers that said we were done. The man holding the papers was from the university's real estate office, which owned our building. He had a thin beard and a crisp university polo shirt tucked in tight to his slim cut jeans. His eyes were squinty behind a pair of frameless glasses. I looked at the paper on top of the pile, which said:

EVICTION NOTICE

It was written in the largest font I have ever seen. People could probably see it from space.

"What's this all about?" I asked.

The man looked down at the gigantic words EVICTION NOTICE. Then he looked back at me. Then he told me what this was all about.

1) The theater was in debt, in excess of $145,000.

2) Randy had mismanaged the budget very badly over the last five years and had missed a lot of grant deadlines that might have kept us afloat.

3) Randy had personally loaned his theater over $75,000, guaranteed against the value of the

property, but now he was out of money.

4) This had been a problem for a long time, and why Randy had never told us about it was anyone's guess.

5) Barring any ability to pay off the debt in full, the university would be forced to demolish the Green Street to make way for a "Residential/Retail establishment."

Once he was done telling me very clearly what this was all about, the man looked at my name tag, which read, "Wendy. Manager," and asked:

"You in charge here, Wendy?"

"I am," I said.

He smiled.

"How old are you?"

"I am very old," was my reply.

He squinted at me with his already squinty eyes. Then he looked around the place, as if for the first time. And it might help to know here that the Green Street was last remodeled in 1935. You know, when Franklin Roosevelt was president. It was originally done in an Art Deco style, which should be really cool. Bold colors and wild geometric shapes. But the glamour had faded over the years.

Like literally faded.

We used to have gold wallpaper, but now most of the

shine had worn off and it looked like faded tinfoil. The cool old light fixtures hadn't been wired in years and collected dust on the walls beneath some bad fluorescents. And the concessions counter looked more like an Old Country Buffet than Radio City Music Hall. In short: The Green Street looked like something that used to be awesome, but was now very not-awesome, and possibly full of black mold.

The man took all this in and then turned back to me.

"Can I ask you a question?" he said.

"Free country," said Griffin from beside me, radiating THC.

I gave him a look. The man's gaze bounced around the room.

"Does anybody actually come to see movies here?" he asked.

He seemed genuinely curious, like the concept was totally mind-blowing to him. Before I could say anything, though, Lucas chimed in from behind the counter, stuffing a handful of popcorn in his mouth straight from the machine.

"We cater to an elite clientele," he said. "True cineastes!"

The man looked at Lucas like he had just blown a particularly foul odor in his direction.

"Ah," he said. "Cineastes."

My feelings at the moment were tough to pin down. On one hand, I wanted to murder Lucas for being such a pretentious ass. But I also wanted to hug him for being so wholly himself in the face of this dude. I wanted to start crying. But I also didn't want to show weakness in front of the enemy. Oddly enough, I also felt like going back into the rat closet. Life had been easier in there.

I was supposed to say something now—that much was clear—but I didn't know what to say. So, I did what I always do when I don't know what to say: I quoted a movie. I have a lot of them memorized. All those post-movie discussions with dad had carved them into my mind.

Here's what I came up with:

"Three weeks from now, I will be harvesting my crops. Imagine where you will be, and it will be so. If you find yourself alone, riding in the green fields with the sun on your face, do not be troubled. For you are in Elysium, and you're already dead!"

The man watched me carefully. Then, after a few seconds, he furrowed his sizable brow, and turned around to walk out the door of the theater. At just that moment, however, Sweet Lou, the organ player happened to be showing up for work. She was very old, and quite large, and she walked with an amazing gold-topped cane. And when the polo man opened the door, Sweet Lou wedged herself past him, stomping out her cigarette on the threadbare carpet of the theater in the process.

"Watch it, honcho," she said.

Then she walked off. The man looked down at the

smoldering cigarette butt, then at Lou disappearing into the theater, paying him absolutely no attention. He left the building then without uttering another word. When he was gone, Lucas walked over and stood beside me.

"Was that a line from *Gladiator*?" he asked.

"Yes," I said. "It was."

"Oh," he said. "Huh."

Behind us at the concession stand, the popcorn was starting to burn.

ETHAN'S GLOSSARY OF FILM TERMS

ENTRY #33

ESTABLISHING SHOT

A long shot at the start of a scene that shows you where you are in time and space.

It might be a spaceship drifting into the frame, a helicopter buzzing over the Gotham skyline.

Or, it might just be a kid going home to a bungalow in Minneapolis—a house that always feels empty now—after a long day at work.

3

I meant to talk to my mom about what was happening that night, but when I got home and tossed my greasy white work shirt in the laundry, she was in the kitchen working on dinner and singing along to the stereo. In the last year or so, she had finally managed to escape the grief that had imprisoned her after my dad was gone. And in addition to finding a new job, and singing more often, she had taken up gourmet cooking.

I realize I should not be complaining about any of this. I don't begrudge my mom happiness, and poached rainbow trout with savoy cabbage is objectively delicious. But, there were just a couple of problems.

1) In her mission to get over the tragedy in her life, she seemed to be forgetting that it had ever happened.

2) I really missed taco night, where we loaded up store-bought taco shells with neon orange ground beef and

shredded lettuce and then ate them while watching the trashiest movie we could find on TV.

Now the TV was downstairs in the basement, far far away from the kitchen table. And ground beef with seasoning packs was forever banned from Mom's kitchen.

"Hey, hey," said my mom, when I stepped into the kitchen. "The workingman is home."

"I am," I said.

"Can you set out the low bowls please and some glasses for wine?"

"Sure," I said, and opened the door to the cabinet near the counter. I pulled out some stacked bowls and wineglasses.

The good side of my mom's gourmand phase is that she let me drink wine with dinner sometimes. Just a glass, but still, if I drank it fast enough, I got the world's tiniest buzz. The bad side was that I couldn't help remembering the things Dad used to make: stuffed peppers with lots of cheese, enormous hamburgers cooked to dangerously low temperatures. Something called Zucchini Slop. The house smelled different these days. It was quieter, too. The pauses between sentences were longer, and I found myself always jumping to fill them.

Mom was dumping out pasta water when I finished with the table, and she appeared before me through a fog of briny steam. Her blond bangs were damp against her forehead. Dad always said she looked like this Italian actress, Monica Vitti, with her long nose and that little gap between her teeth. But to me, she just looked like my mom.

I could smell the clams and garlic and knew we were having spaghetti vongole, which was her specialty.

"How was the theater today?" she asked.

"Fine," I said. "Sweet Lou fell asleep at the organ again."

"Of course she did."

"Her head landed right on D-flat during the opening credits of the matinee. A woman screamed."

Mom laughed, but not the way she used to. This was just a soft chuckle. A half laugh at best. She wasn't a huge fan of my extra responsibilities at the Green Street. She thought I should be concentrating on retaking the SATs or looking into humanitarian work if I was planning to take a "gap year."

That's what she called my plan for next year. A gap year. Even though the word "gap" implied a space between things, and I had no idea what the next thing would be. Can there be a gap with nothing on the other side? A cliff year?

I had graduated early from high school thanks to a boatload of AP credits from the good old days. Mom was surprisingly cool with my early graduation, but her pride had turned quickly to anxiety when I showed no immediate interest in college.

"Can you finish chopping this basil?" she asked now, and pointed toward a cutting board. I walked over and picked up her ridiculously expensive Japanese chef's knife. It was sharp enough to take off a digit if you didn't concentrate.

"How about a chiffonade?" she said.

She had been trying for a year to teach me some knife skills. A chiffonade, for those of you who don't work at a Michelin-starred restaurant, is a cut that makes perfect little herb strings. You do it by folding the herbs and making tiny slices, and it takes about a hundred forevers unless you're a pro.

I am not a pro.

Still, I lined up the basil, folded it over, and started the intricate work of slicing through the herbs to the rib.

"Guess who I saw today at the farmer's market?" she asked.

She was stirring her sauce into the pasta now, her newly toned arm whirling in circles.

"Roger Deakins?"

She stopped stirring.

"Who?"

"Roger Deakins. The fourteen-time Academy Award–nominated cinematographer who worked on such films as *No Country for Old Men* and *The Shawshank Redemption*."

"No," my mom said, "not him."

"Oh," I said, "who then?"

I finished one side of the basil leaves and flipped them over.

"Trinity Allen," she said.

I stopped the knife before almost cutting off the tip of my thumb.

"As in . . ." I said.

"As in Raina's mom," she said.

"Mmm," I said.

I was no longer chiffonading. I had not heard either of the names my mom had just uttered in a very long time. Well, I had read about them on websites, but I had not heard them spoken aloud. And this was because the owners of those names used to live nearby us, but now they did not. They used to be frequent topics of conversation and now they were not. And most importantly, I used to think I would marry Raina Allen, perhaps in a Scottish castle overlooking some moors, whatever those are, but now I did not.

"She's coming home for a while," my mom said.

"She as in . . ."

"She as in Raina. The girl you wanted to marry in a Scottish castle."

"Who told you about that?"

"You wrote it on your wall in Magic Marker," she said.

I poured myself a tall glass of wine.

"Hey! Easy tiger," said Mom, pointing at my glass. "Pour some of that back."

I sighed and dumped half my glass into hers, spilling a citrusy splash on the tablecloth. I watched it soak into the fibers.

"I thought she was shooting the sequel to that dystopic cats thing," I said.

My mom grabbed my ill-chopped basil and garnished a few perfectly swirled pasta towers.

"She was replaced," my mom said. "Apparently something didn't go well. I think she's having a tough time. Maybe you should give her a call."

I watched the steam rise off the pasta in front of me, but I was no longer hungry. I got up and took my wine to my bedroom where I lay down on my bed and turned on a movie by one of my dad's favorite directors. Federico Fellini. This one was called *8 1/2*. From what I could tell, it was about a dashing man who wanders around, ignoring beautiful women for three hours. I tried my best to experience his sophisticated boredom, but my heart was beating so fast, I thought it might explode.

4

I fell in love with Raina Allen the day she brought her diorama to class in third grade. It was a project for the school science fair. We had been assigned mandatory projects in November, a series of boring topics that mostly had to do with measuring precipitation levels and learning about the various flatulent land mammals of our region. But Raina had raised her hand when we got our projects and said, "Mrs. Boswell, I don't want to be a pain, but I think it would be better if I did a diorama."

And Mrs. Boswell, who spent a decent amount of time squashing the dreams of Raina and others like her, froze for a minute. I could see even with my puny third-grade powers of perception that she was on the verge of saying "Nope. Sorry. Precipitation levels for you." But maybe because she was distracted, or in a rare good mood, or bored out of her mind at the thought of seeing another graph of

Minnesota snowfall, said, "Okay, Raina. But don't make me regret this decision."

And Raina meanwhile had this look on her face like: *Okay, Mrs. Boswell, you can send your teacher threats my way, but I AM going to make you regret your decision because this diorama is going to BLOW YOUR FUCKING MIND.* And sure enough, when Raina brought her project to our pathetic little science fair in the cafeteria on a slushy December morning, it was nothing short of astonishing.

Imagine, if you will, a large box.

Now imagine eyeholes cut into this box.

I can see you being underwhelmed, but stay with me.

Because now you walk up to this large, unsuspecting box and adjust your face so that your eyes line up perfectly with those eyeholes. You blink a few times, and it takes a second for your eyes to adjust to the dim red light that has been switched on inside. But when your vision clears you see a battle between two 12,000-year-old woolly mammoths rendered in photo-realist detail.

There they are: constructed in clay, frozen mid-attack, their tusks tangled together in a grapple for dominance. One of them is falling down, but he hasn't quite reached the ground yet, his mouth constricted in an angry mammoth death grimace. The other lunges forward, his leg pierced from a prior attack from the now-victim. In the background is a watching herd of tiny mammoths surrounded by a canopy of giant dinosaur-times ferns. And in the sky above them, a red sun blazing.

That is what I saw inside that box.

And what I felt was joy. Not admiration, at least not right away. Not jealousy. Just pure unadulterated joy. The box was like a movie. A movie that didn't move. And it elicited the same joy I would feel later when I watched the Millennium Falcon jump to light speed for the first time, or the DeLorean disappear at the end of *Back to the Future* or later still when Ben and Elaine are running from the church in *The Graduate*, stumbling onto a bus completely unsure of what's coming next, with only their flawed love to guide them. The kind of joy that plucks you, temporarily, out of your life.

And when I finally pulled away from that diorama and locked in on Raina's expectant eyes, I was speechless. What I wanted to say was: *I love you, Raina. And while I don't really know what moors are, I am going to find out someday and then we are going to get married on some.* But once I found myself able to actually utter words again, I think I said something like: "Cool mammoths." To which Raina nodded, and then went back to being effortlessly awesome.

And that was that.

It was my first experience with unrequited love. It would not be my last. But for the moment, Raina Allen could do no wrong in my eyes. I must have realized on some level that she did not just exist for me. Her role was not to make my life awesome. Her mammoths were not created just to expand my sense of wonder. She made them for herself. She made them for the progress of third-grade science.

No matter the reason, I just knew I wanted to be near her.

So for the rest of elementary school, I watched her from afar, occasionally joining one of her elaborate role-playing games at recess, happy to be given the part of the robot dog in a sci-fi epic or, more than once, "bumbling squire" to the first female Knight of the Round Table. She rarely said my name, and each year on Valentine's Day, when I chose the best cartoon franchise valentine for her and tucked it into her cardboard mailbox, I allowed myself the hope that she might finally reciprocate my feelings of adoration. But her valentines were never personalized, and she never let me know she had received mine. And that's the way things went until we left the halls of Hillcrest Elementary.

In sixth grade, though, things began to change.

In grade school, Raina had held us in sway with her strange ways. No one cared that she cut off her bangs with safety scissors in art class. Or that she ate ketchup with a spoon. No one cared because weird was cool in grade school. Weird was fun. Weird made the games better and the days go faster.

Then, in junior high, suddenly weird took a fall from

grace. Weird was no longer cool. Weird was wrong and bad and embarrassing. At least according to the eighth-grade overlords who controlled everything with their perfectly timed eye rolls and shrugs and new boobs and amazingly fragrant lip gloss. They took one look at Raina with her messy blond hair and boys' shoes, and they decided that she was anonymous.

Anonymous like me.

We met again in gym class, the great equalizer. Well, we met outside gym class technically, both of us using the same evasion tactic of a bathroom break. The hallway outside the sweat-fogged gymnasium had two drinking fountains side by side, and we both took a drink and then hesitated to go back in where the terrible sounds of a game called Prison Ball were echoing around. It doesn't matter if you know what Prison Ball is. It has the word "prison" in it. That should give you the gist.

"Ethan, right?" she said.

And then I'm pretty sure I choked on some water I was trying to swallow.

"Yeah," I squeaked.

"What happened?" she asked.

"Oh. Some water went down the wrong tube, but I think I'm okay."

"No," she said. "I mean how did we get here? How did *this* happen?"

I listened to one of my Prison Ball teammates screaming like a Viking raider inside the gym. I didn't know how to answer Raina's question.

She continued: "Last year we were playing Oregon Trail and eating cupcakes on people's birthdays. And now . . . all of this."

She pointed at the halls, a bewildered look in her eye.

"Yeah," I said. "I get what you mean."

She looked at me, waiting for more.

"I mean. It's even worse than everyone said. It's like *Battle Royale* or something," I said.

She had been nodding, but now she stopped.

"What's *Battle Royale*?"

"Oh, it's this film by Kinji Fukasaka about these kids who have to fight to death for the Japanese government. Early on, someone gets a knife to the head for whispering. It's intense."

Her face was unreadable. She seemed to really look at me then. She took in my skinny legs and too-tight gym shirt. My haircut that looked accidental at best.

"How are you going to make it, Ethan?" she asked.

It hadn't occurred to me to ask that question yet. And being asked directly shook me to the very moorings of my soul.

"I don't know," I said. "I don't really have a strategy or anything."

She thought for a minute, and I could see her wondering if she should mention the next thing at all.

"Listen," she said finally, "this might be your thing. It might not. But my mom's signing me up for acting classes on Saturdays at the Community Playhouse. It seems pretty cool. They have real costumes and everything. But so far, we don't have any boys for the plays. I mean, I'm down for playing a boy if I have to, but I'd like an element of realism if possible. Anyway . . ."

I stared at her.

"You think I should join?" I asked inanely.

"Well . . . if it's your thing."

"I don't know what my thing is," I said. "I might not have a thing."

"Oh," she said. "That's sad."

I looked at her. Her eyes were already looking past me.

"Listen," she said. "Come if you want, or you know . . . don't."

Then she walked off toward the cafeteria, and I never saw her in gym class again. Later, I found out she faked a back problem. But I did see her at the Playhouse, which would miraculously bring us closer together for a short time before pushing us as far apart as we could possibly get.

ETHAN'S GLOSSARY OF FILM TERMS

ENTRY #76

META-FILM

A film about a film. Or a film that acknowledges it's a film.

You know, something self-aware where characters break the fourth wall to talk to the viewer directly (what a terrible idea, right?).

Think Ferris Bueller giving you advice about faking sick or Amélie talking about how she likes to watch people's faces in a darkened theater.

"That's so meta!"

I've heard Lucas say from time to time, usually with a satisfied smile on his face, as if he alone has caught the reference.

"Is it?" I've been known to say back, "is it really *so meta*?"

5

Let's pause here for a quick thought experiment.

I want you to think about how much you used to go to the movies. Like when you were a kid. Or maybe just five years ago. How many times a week? A month?

I'll wait a minute. . . .

Done?

Okay, now think about how much you go these days.

If you're like most people, it's probably less. Don't worry. I'm not judging you. Well . . . actually, I am kind of judging you, but I also get it. The times, they are a changing and stuff. There are streaming services. And illegal sites. And TVs are equipped with super-duper surround sound and HD and they're curved and made of magic liquid pixels or something. So, why would you go and pay fifteen bucks— less at the Green Street, but still—to sit with a bunch of coughing strangers fiddling on their phones watching something you could pirate off the Internet for free?

And if you *were* going to go to the movies for once, why would you come to our un-air-conditioned, one screen theater, with sticky seats and the perpetual smell of cigarette smoke in the wallpaper, to watch a movie by an obscure director that probably came out at least fifteen years ago, and maybe no one even saw then? Why would you take two hours of your life, hours that could be spent in any manner of other ways and subject yourself to Lucas's pretentious sneer, or Griffin's stoned indifference, or my obvious desperation?

You wouldn't. I get it. You just wouldn't.

But here's why maybe you should:

To avoid being super average and boring.

I'll explain.

Basically, I think it's easy to go through life just doing the same things everyone else does.

Hey, have you seen the popular show everyone's watching?

Yes, as a matter of fact I have. Because I crave social acceptance.

But have you seen the latest one-hundred-million-dollar movie based on a comic book franchise?

Yes, of course. It is my duty as a citizen to my corporate lords.

But here's the thing . . . if you only see the same movies

that everyone else does, if you only watch the same shows and read the same books, and listen to the same music that everyone else does, then you're only ever going to have the same ideas as everyone else. You're only going to see the world the way everyone else does. And sure there's a reason people like those things. They're entertaining and "fun." But they're also probably made to appeal to every single person on earth, and so they're also kind of bland and familiar and unchallenging. The Arby's of cultural offerings.

Do you feel like beating me up yet?

It's okay. I feel like beating me up sometimes.

But before you completely tune me out, let me paint a different picture. Just briefly. Let's say, for the sake of my thought experiment, that you come to the Green Street instead. Let's say you come to a showing of *Rubber*, a movie by the French director Quentin Dupieux. *Rubber* is a movie about a car tire that comes to life and develops powers of telekinesis, which it uses to blow up people's heads.

Wanna see it?

Sure you do! It's kind of a house favorite around the Green Street, and Randy once got pissed at us when he found out it was the Midnight Movie two Saturdays in a row. But anyway, I don't want to claim that watching this tire (who is named Robert by the way. How awesome is that?) explode a dude's head at a gas station is necessarily going to change your life. But you might be surprised.

For instance, there's this scene where the tire is rolling through the desert and comes across a bunch of guys burning huge piles of car tires. Like one after the next. And the tire just stands there watching it all, taking it in. And when I first watched this moment, I had been laughing through the movie up to this point. Because, I mean, it's a movie about a tire! And the tire murders a rabbit! But, when I saw this part, I started to feel something else. My eyes blurred and I realized I was crying. It was tire genocide, and the director, this guy Dupieux, had made me care about the humanity of a rubber tire. And how often does that happen in your life? How often do you get startled out of your everyday worries and break down and cry over a tire?

Probably not often, right?

Probably you're going to go through your whole life without having that experience. But maybe you should have it. Maybe you should come to a tiny decaying movie theater and cry with the weirdos. Maybe then the Green Street would not be on the verge of turning into a Retail/Residential space. A Retail/Residential space where college kids who are too spoiled to live in the regular dorms can eat a gourmet sushi burrito before taking the elevator up to their penthouse suites to smoke artisanal marijuana and play video games on a projection TV.

I swear I'm not bitter.

And I know I'm not going to change all of contemporary culture overnight. And I'm probably not going to take down mass media or capitalism anytime soon. Frankly, that sounds like a lot of work, and I could never even be bothered to learn trigonometry at anything more than a C level.

What I needed to help me out of this current crisis was a more realistic plan.

What I needed was to see the Oracle.

6

The Oracle could be found at all times in the projection booth of the Green Street Cinema. Rumor had it she only left to buy fermented probiotic beverages. Her name is Angela, but everybody calls her Anjo. If I had to guess, I would say she's thirty. But it's a tough call. Her eyes look super bright behind her signature cat's-eye glasses, but when she takes her hair out of its thick braid she looks much older all of a sudden.

I was told when I was first hired at the Green Street that she spent most of her twenties getting paid to do medical studies. She moved into hospitals and tried new pharmaceuticals to see if they had side effects. Some of them did. Some of them didn't. Does she still have side effects? I don't know. But there is definitely something a little glazed about her. Her pupils have never quite un-dilated from her years of prescriptions. She also happens to be one of the most genuine people I know. And one of the smartest.

Sadly, I didn't see her much. She liked to hide in the booth, and I never pretended to be her boss. I gave her a list of the film prints we needed for the month, and she tracked them down and had them sent to the theater. All I ever saw were the invoices. Then, right on time every day, she would fire up the projector and show the films without any trouble. When we were done with them, she'd ship them back. She was reliable. She'd been there since the early days, and part of me felt like she always would be.

I walked up the old stairs to her booth, holding a Green Goddess salad from the restaurant down the street, which I knew to be her special occasion dinner, a small offering for her counsel. When I reached the door and knocked, it only took a second before she pulled it open and put a finger to her lips. She waved me in, and I tiptoed into the dim room, which she had spent years turning into her own personal lady cave.

There was a mini-refrigerator and an old microwave. There were some extra clothes in stacked cardboard boxes. And in the corner, there was her shrine to Steve McQueen, the handsome sixties leading man, nicknamed the "King of Cool." On the poster hanging above a single burning prayer candle, he wore aviator shades, with a cigarette dangling from his lower lip, suspended there for all of eternity.

Anjo took the salad from my hands without comment. I

opened my mouth to say something about burning candles and flammable film stock, but she frowned at me.

"Shhhhhhh," she said. "This is the most beautiful part."

She directed my attention to the rectangular peephole where the light of the projector flickered toward the screen below. As I got closer, I heard the flutter of Vicky, the house projector (a Victoria 35mm), as the film spooled through. On the screen below, there was a silent film playing. We'd been doing mostly Charlie Chaplin and Buster Keaton on Saturday afternoons lately. The old scratchy prints were really beautiful and you could always count on a few old-timers to wander in with their grandchildren.

In this one, Buster Keaton played a cameraman, trying to impress a woman who works for the News Reels at MGM. Sweet Lou provided the meandering score on her organ, her bifocals reflecting the warm light of the screen. The film was at the part where Buster has just been chewed out for loading his film wrong and losing his footage. Then the woman he loves comes out to give him a pep talk in the hall. He tries to hide behind his camera, but she leans around and puts a hand on his shoulder. The title card comes up with the dialogue.

"Don't be discouraged. No one would ever amount to anything, if he didn't try."

The woman shows him how to use the camera, and when he turns around they almost kiss. Sweet Lou's organ playing reached a crescendo, only to fall off when the kiss didn't happen. Then the actors just stand there in the dazzling light of the old black-and-white film.

I looked over at Anjo. She had taken off her glasses, and I could see the light from the projector strobing in her wide pupils. When the scene ended, she wiped a tear away and plopped down on a beat-up futon she had scavenged from the dorm Dumpsters on move-out day.

"It's a tragedy," she said in her soft, calm voice, opening the to-go container that held her salad.

"What is?"

"Once sound came to the movies, nobody cared about him anymore. He was stuck making cheesy low-budget stuff. He disappeared in the name of progress."

She forked a bite of salad in her mouth, and stared into space.

"Anjo, I have to tell you something," I said.

A desk lamp shone on her face from a nearby table.

"I already know about the eviction," she said.

My mouth fell open.

"How?"

She closed her eyes and pressed her palms together beneath her chin.

"The Oracle hears all," she said.

I felt myself blushing. I had no idea she knew about her nickname.

"How long before the hour of our fate, fearless leader?" she said.

I sighed.

"The end of the month."

She clucked her tongue and took a long breath.

"It's a big debt, Ethan," she said.

Anjo was the only one who still called me by my given name. She'd worked here when I used to come with my dad, when I was just a volunteer. She used to see me, down below her perch, sitting next to my dad, trying to make sense of experimental Swedish cinema. She had admired Dad, like everyone else who knew him. Which is probably why she let me come up here to chat.

"I don't suppose you have any amazing ideas," I said.

"Oh," she said. "I get it. This salad wasn't free."

In the theater below, a smattering of laughs rang out. Keaton must have taken a pratfall. Anjo got up from her chair and opened the door to her mini-fridge. She pulled out a jar of strange green juice and poured a little in a plastic cup.

"Here," she said. "Drink this down, boss-man."

"What is it?" I asked.

"Absinthe," she said.

I held it farther away from myself.

"Relax. It's wheatgrass juice." She smiled. "Cleanses the liver."

I took a hesitant sip. It tasted like lawn clippings. Anjo started to talk.

"In the nineteen thirties, Buster was at his lowest. He had just been fired by MGM. His wife had divorced him and he couldn't even see his sons. His kind of humor was out of style. Everybody wanted screwball comedies, with fast-talking wise guys. Like I said, the only movies he made were low budget, B-grade things where he was forced to become a kind of caricature of himself, rehashing old gags. But here's the thing: If you watch the movies, you can still see flashes of brilliance. Even though he's been backed into a corner by studio bosses, and forced to humiliate himself in bad movies, the innocence and optimism is still there. Even though he probably felt defeated, they couldn't rob him of his spark. They couldn't completely break him."

I looked down into my shot of wheatgrass.

"Bottoms up," she said, and touched my hand.

I drank it and for a moment I felt a little better. Like I'd downed a magic potion. But soon enough, the feeling started to dissipate.

"So, what does that mean for the theater?" I asked.

Anjo walked to the projector and a made a few small adjustments. Her glasses slipped down her nose, and she nudged them back up with a thumb.

"The Oracle has spoken," she said.

ETHAN'S GLOSSARY OF FILM TERMS

ENTRY #3

CLOSE-UP

Okay, everybody knows this one.

But I'm still going to talk about it because
I like how honest a close-up is.

There are all kinds of theories about what
they're supposed to do. Show heightened
emotion. Capture details. Make us bond
with a character.

But can't we all just admit that part of the
reason we go to the movies is to look at nice
faces. And not just any nice faces. Enormous
nice faces taking up the whole screen, looking
down at us like gods.

7

Everything changed when Raina was discovered.

And I know what you're thinking: Is anyone really "discovered" anymore? Is that still a thing? Short answer: yes. But it didn't happen in Minnesota.

Raina had begged her mom for years to take her to New York to see some Broadway musicals. At some point, Trinity finally relented. So Raina was standing outside a theater, wearing a dress with cats on it, when a nondescript middle-aged man walked up to her and gave her a card. Her mom was inside at the will-call window, trying to get them last-minute seats to *Cabaret*, and so Raina was all alone.

The way she described it to me was that it should have been really creepy. She was in eighth grade. She was a late-bloomer, and not necessarily a knockout by most people's standards. But there she was, her dark blond hair in two long braids, wearing her mom's oversize sunglasses and a cat dress. And the man stopped in front of her and smiled.

"I never do this," he said.

And Raina, who had seen her beautiful mother harassed by strange men on too many occasions said, "Then don't do it."

Instead of walking away, though, the guy just laughed.

"Where did you get that dress?" he asked.

Again, he was talking to an eighth grader. Which is definitely kind of skeevy. But it was broad daylight, and he wasn't leering at her. He just seemed curious. So Raina took a chance and told the truth.

"Walmart," she said.

She looked down at herself. The dress was yellow and sleeveless with a print of cats wearing glasses on it. She had worn it because they were supposed to see *Cats* today, which she knew was a little corny and childish, but it also struck her as kind of perfect. How often do you get to wear cats to *Cats*? Her mom, however, had messed something up online and there were no seats for them. So, it was to be *Cabaret* instead. Still, she wasn't going to change her clothes at that point. She was committed to the cat dress.

"Have you ever done any modeling?" he asked.

Now it was Raina's turn to laugh.

"Yeah, man. Didn't you see me in *Teen Vogue* last week? I was wearing Gucci slippers."

She was still giggling when her mom came out of the theater and took a protective step in front of her daughter. She put a hand inside her purse where Raina knew she kept her enormous canister of pepper spray.

"What's going on here? Who are you?"

The man put his hands up in the air as if he were being mugged. Then, slowly, he reached into the front pocket of his very expensive Oxford shirt and produced a business card.

"Paul Houston," he said. "I'm a casting director. And I'd like to introduce your daughter to a director."

He waited patiently for Raina and her mom to Google his agency on their phones, find a matching picture, and see his client list. It was an impressive list.

"How long are you in town?" he asked as they finished their detective work.

"Two more days," said Trinity, softened a little by what she'd found.

"Any chance you can extend that?" he asked. "At my expense, of course."

Trinity looked at Raina. Raina looked back at her mother.

A week later, she had an agent, and she was preparing to audition for a teen blockbuster about a nerdy girl who has to save the world from a time-traveling evil cat. She beat out every young actress you've ever heard of for the role.

How did she do it?

By thinking that it was never going to happen. Instead of preparing, she just went in and played herself. She ad-libbed a few bad jokes. She asked a few questions about her character. Then she realistically mimed hanging from a cliff while trying to keep a rescued, magical kitten in the pocket of a sweatshirt.

A year after that, she was famous.

For a while we stayed in touch. I still had her phone number, which became a well-kept secret, and I knew which social media accounts were the real ones. She lived in California now, and when we spoke, she'd mostly ask me about details from home. The polenta fries at Muddy Waters. The art installations on the ice at Lake Harriet. What play they were doing at the Community Playhouse. She seemed genuinely interested. Like maybe she really missed being a regular person in Minnesota with a cheap haircut and a gym locker. Though I couldn't imagine why that would be true.

I tried not to ask about her new celebrity status too much, but it was hard to resist. I'd never met anyone famous before, unless you counted the washed-up celebrities who turned up at the mall once in a while to launch their shoe lines.

I'd write:

When you go on a talk show, do they really have baskets of free stuff back there? Can you take anything you want? Is it considered unprofessional to eat the whole muffin basket, or to take it home like a doggie bag?

I'd get a reply a few days later.

Swag Bags are real! I don't care if it's
unprofessional. When a muffin is free,
I eat the muffin. Are you still working at
the Green Street?

Every once in a while, we'd talk on the phone, but hearing her voice was a little too much for me. In the end, I was stuck in the position of being genuinely happy for her, while simultaneously mourning the loss of my only real friend. You can see why I could fake it better in texts. On the phone, it was hard to keep my voice from quavering. And I was always on the verge of saying "Come home. Come home. Come home."

Then my dad died.

And she didn't come home.

In her defense, it would have been nearly impossible. She was shooting in Greenland. But she could have come later. It still would have helped. She didn't do that, either. She never came back to see me. In fact, she didn't even contact me. The worst thing imaginable had happened, and my best friend wasn't there for me. It was beyond my understanding.

After that, I stopped texting. And I tried to move on. A year passed. Then another. I was put in charge of the Green Street. And, aside from the occasional Google alert, I tried not to think about her. In fact, I had almost successfully transformed her from best friend/unrequited love to pop-culture trivia when my mom told me she was back in town and that I should reach out because she was in trouble.

But who wasn't in trouble? That's what I wanted to know.

Life, it seemed to me, was mostly trouble. Sacred movie theaters got eviction notices from guys with tight shirts. Friendships ended as quickly as they began. People died when you didn't want them to die. It was, so often, a low-down, disappointing business as far as I could tell. Which is why I spent most of my time watching movies.

A text came through on my phone now. It was from a number I didn't recognize. But I hadn't made any new friends lately, so there was really only one person it could be.

Ethan, it read. **Are you there?**

8

There was only one thing to do:

I walked into the rat closet and sat on an industrial-size box of Sour Patch Kids. This was my thinking spot. I chose the Sour Patch Kids because they were an odd phenomenon to me. Not too many people ate them outside of the movies. And, yet, they weren't really a classic theater candy like Junior Mints or Dots. They sold just enough to justify their presence in the case, but no more. They were the modest survivors of the theater candy world.

They were also the only candy the rats wanted nothing to do with.

I opened the big box and took out a package. I ripped it open.

"Why don't you want these?" I asked any giant rats who might be lurking.

I dumped a few of the crusted gummies in my mouth.

And as my whole tongue lit up with a thousand flames of sour-sweetness, I understood why they might go neglected.

"Fine," I said. "More for me."

I tossed another handful in my mouth and pressed call back on my phone.

The ringing seemed to last forever. One long tone after the other, vibrating for years in my ear. I didn't hang up, though. And just when I was sure I would be listening to that sound forever, I heard her voice.

"You have the same number," she said.

I was still chewing candy globs, and it took me a minute to speak.

"It's true," I said eventually. "Everything about me is the same. My number. My blood type. My inability to ignore a message from you."

I barely knew what I was saying. The last time I had heard her voice was in a movie. Now when she spoke, it sounded like it could be in the room with me.

"My mom was happy to see your mom yesterday."

She was silent for a few seconds. I looked around the darkened storage closet.

"She said your mom was looking good. Like she was a whole new person or something."

"Yeah," I said. "She's living her *best life*, in quotation marks. I guess it's good. She smiles more."

"And what about you?" she asked. "Are you living your *best life* in quotation marks?"

I could hear a sly smile in her voice.

"I think I am living my best life in finger quotes," I said.

There was another silence then, and I heard Lucas and Griffin arguing about something at the concession stand. Lucas kept saying, "That being said!" I assumed it was movie-related. The world could be ending and the two of them would still be arguing about which Coen Brothers film was the most underrated (*Miller's Crossing*).

"You're not going to ask why I'm home?" she said.

I was quiet.

"I went AWOL," she blurted.

It took me a second to catch up.

"What do you mean? You ran away from home?"

"No," she said. "Worse. I ran away from set."

I adjusted myself on my giant box of candy. She spoke again.

"I was supposed to be filming in like fifteen minutes. They had this huge scene set up, and I just sort of walked away from my trailer and didn't tell anyone."

"Why?" I asked.

She didn't answer.

"Where did you go?"

She sighed.

"What?" I asked. "How embarrassing could it be?"

"I went to Dairy Queen."

I couldn't help myself. I laughed.

"I guess that's a pretty good choice," I said. "Was it a Brazier?"

No response for a few seconds. Then:

"What's a Brazier?"

"Are you kidding me right now?"

"No."

"You've been away from the Midwest too long."

"Probably," she said. "What's a Brazier?"

"A Brazier is a Dairy Queen with a grill where you can get burgers and stuff. It's way better than a regular Dairy Queen because, you know: burgers."

"You mean a Grill and Chill?" she said.

"A what?" I said.

She sighed.

"It wasn't a Brazier."

"Bummer."

She was silent on the line.

"Sorry," I said. "Continue with your story."

"There isn't really a story."

"So, you just went to Dairy Queen and came back? That's not going AWOL. That's going to Dairy Queen."

"I went to Dairy Queen for ten hours."

"Oh."

"My mom reported me missing. And they found me at the Culver City Mall. I was crying I guess."

"For ten hours?"

"I don't remember."

"You don't remember if you were crying for ten hours?"

"I don't remember any of it. They told me about it later."

"I see."

"So, I'm home now. Resting, in quotation marks. It isn't very restful, actually."

"What about your movie?"

I heard a muffled voice in the background, and the rustle of what must have been Raina's hair against the phone.

"Sorry, I have to go now, Ethan. But you should come over some time. I'd like to see you."

"Where are you staying?"

"Our old house. Mom never sold it."

Long uncomfortable pause.

"Good-bye, Ethan."

I tried to say good-bye, but what came out was:

"Why?"

At first I wasn't sure if she'd hung up. But then she spoke:

"Why what?"

I steeled myself with a breath.

"Why do you want to see me?"

She didn't say anything, so I spoke again:

"We haven't really been talking."

"Maybe that's why I want to see you. Part of it anyway."

I wasn't sure what to say.

"I have to go," she said. "Come by if you want. Or, you know . . ."

"Don't?" I said.

"Yeah."

Then she hung up the phone. I looked around the room. My eyes had adjusted more to the light, and now that I could see the walls, I felt a sense of claustrophobia. Then I heard a scratching sound coming from the box next to me. I yanked it off the rickety metal shelf and saw a flash of tail before it was gone.

The door swung open. And I heard a shrill scream.

"Ah. Christ, Wendy. You scared the hell out of me!"

Lucas shielded himself from me then reached in and grabbed a single box of Milk Duds. He inspected it for rat damage, his dark brown eyes roving over the cardboard. He was about to go back to whatever he was doing when I spoke up.

"What do you think about all this?" I said.

"About you hiding in the storage closet? I'm a little worried."

"The eviction," I said.

He looked away. The bangs of his asymmetrical black hair dipped over his left eye. Then he smiled and looked back at me.

"I think we need to make a stand, *Die Hard* style. You, me, and Anjo barefoot in the ducts, picking off the real estate office guys, one by one!"

He did his best Hans Gruber: "Now I haff a machine gun. Ho. Ho. Ho."

"No Griffin?"

"Griffin couldn't find his way out of a tube sock. Plus, he'd sell us out for a burrito in two minutes. I imagine Anjo would be lethal though. Like *La Femme Nikita*. You know?"

"Uh-huh."

I watched him as he continued to daydream, running a hand through his hair.

"You realize it's really going to happen, though. Right?" I said.

"What do you mean?"

"Like, this is *not* actually a movie. We're not going to kill the bad guys. They're just going to come and take this place away from us because we don't have one hundred and fifty thousand dollars. And nobody wants us here anymore."

"The regulars do."

"They're not enough. Everybody else wants condos. And a noodle bar. Advancement of the species."

He nodded.

"And then, when it happens, we won't be here anymore getting paid to have these conversations."

His eyes avoided mine. He rattled the box of Milk Duds in his hand.

"Then you better do something," he said.

I stood up from my box.

"Why me?" I asked. "Why can't you figure it out? Or . . . I don't know, everyone else?"

Lucas looked at me incredulously, like he couldn't believe that I'd ask such an obvious question.

"Because you're the manager, Wendy," he said. "Now manage!"

I watched him carefully to see if he was messing with me. He didn't seem to be. But I couldn't think of anything to say so the moment faded.

"Hey," he said. "I forgot to tell you. This film blog I read said Raina Allen from the Time Zap movies was at Muddy Waters yesterday. Didn't you used to know that girl?"

I waited an uncomfortable length of time before answering.

"I did," I said finally.

He waited a moment to see if I had anything more to add. I did not.

"Okay," he said. "Good talk, boss."

He took the Milk Duds with him and gently closed the closet door, leaving me, as usual, in the dark.

ETHAN'S GLOSSARY OF FILM TERMS

MISE-EN-SCÈNE

A French term meaning "pretentious."

Just kidding. It means "placing on the stage."

It comes originally from the theater and refers to the complete visual effect of everything we see in the frame.

Costumes. Props. Backdrops. Bodies. All the visual components.

I don't use this one too often. It's hard to get away with casual French in daily conversation, at least around Griffin and Lucas. But I think about it sometimes. Mostly when I'm places I'm not supposed to be.

Like: everything was perfect in the Mise-en-scène until Ethan showed up.

9

The Community Playhouse smelled like mothballs. At least, that's how I remember it. Probably, it still does, but I've barely set foot in the building since Raina left, so I don't know for sure. The smell was from all the boxes of old costumes. Musty leather jackets from *Grease*. Wigs from *The Crucible*. Codpieces from *The Tempest* (okay, I made that one up). I sat on the floor in a black box theater on that first Saturday after Raina's invitation while all the theater kids made inside jokes and sang songs from musicals with the lyrics changed.

"Ikea, I just met a girl at Ikea!"

"Oh my God, shut up, Claire! People are going to think you're so high."

These were not my people. Movies and theater were two different mediums with two different brands of nerd. Film nerds were introverts, observers mostly, who sat at the back of theaters and stayed through the credits. Theater nerds sang in the shower and started backrub trains after putting on their stage makeup. Neither of us really had any social skills to speak of, but there was so much extroverted energy in the room that Saturday, it felt like the walls were closing in on me.

Then Raina showed up.

She walked calmly across the theater and sat down beside me on the dusty floor. Her dirty blond hair was tucked into a messy ponytail.

"Hey, Ethan," she said.

Then she turned toward the teacher.

"Oh, hey," I said, real nonchalant.

And that was enough to sustain me over the next hour. An hour in which I participated in all manner of energetic "warm-ups." I pretended to be a tiny seed growing into a towering willow tree. I played improv freeze tag and could never think of a line. And I finished with a yoga exercise where I was asked to paint the ceiling with my mind. It was kind of like a series of personal nightmares, only I was awake and my parents were paying for them.

Our teacher, Mrs. Salazar, had been a stage actress in New York for a few years when she was young before returning to Minnesota to raise a family and teach these classes, I guess. She liked to drop names that no one had ever heard of. She had frizzy dark hair, and a hint of a mustache. But when something made her laugh, she threw her head back and brayed. I liked her passion. Then at the end of the first class, she handed out scripts.

"We're going to be doing scenes from *Oliver* this fall," she said. "Auditions are next week. Prepare a song!"

My heart shriveled in my chest. I held the photocopied script in my hand, but I couldn't really see it through blurred vision. Outside, I followed Raina to the parking lot and tapped her on the shoulder.

"So, um. I'm quitting this," I said. "Thanks for inviting me, though."

"You're not quitting," she said.

Her hair was down and she chewed carelessly on a strand.

"I don't have a choice," I said. "I don't know how to prepare a song. I don't know how to sing a song. Let alone *prepare* one."

"Relax," she said. "Just listen to a song on YouTube and sing along until it's memorized."

"I'm not sure that's gonna do it."

She looked at me directly then, her eyes blinking in confusion.

"Good God, man! Do I have to spell this out for you?"

I stared at her, slack-jawed.

"If you didn't notice, there were like two other boys in that whole room today. Two. Total. You're statistically guaranteed a part. You could whistle a song out your ass. All you have to do is show up."

Parents were pulling into the lot now, jockeying for position in the narrow lanes. I saw my mom in our rusty Volvo, searching me out. She could never find me in situations like these, which only confirmed to me that I was the type of person who was not meant for the spotlight.

"But if I get a part," I said, "I'll have to perform it in public."

"True," she said. "That's what acting is."

"I don't like doing things in public," I said. "I don't like doing most things in private."

Raina scanned the row of cars for her ride. She looked at me again and sighed.

"Listen," she said. "We used to play games on the playground, right? When we were in school?"

I nodded. I was surprised that she remembered.

"And you were always down for that. I could get you to do anything. Even if no one else wanted to play."

I had never thought of it that way, that she might have needed me at times. I tried not to get distracted.

"I was a kid," I said.

She closed her eyes and took a breath.

"You still are."

I felt an irrational jump of anger. I knew she was trying to make a point, but I didn't want her to see me as a kid.

"Why do you care so much about this?" I said. "I don't need you to babysit me."

A lie.

She looked at me for a moment. And I thought, temporarily, that she might be deciding whether or not to hit me. Then she took a breath.

"Look, Ethan. I'm not trying to babysit you. I just thought it would be fun to do this with you. Okay? That's why I asked."

I was silent now. She was not.

"I asked you to come so we could hang out. So I could have a friend here. Do you understand?"

My heart was in my throat now, and I could feel my face flush. To avoid meeting Raina's eyes, I looked around at the other kids leaving.

"These people aren't your friends?" I asked.

"Nope," she said. "They never talk to me. I'm pretty sure they go to fancy theater camp in the summer together. So, could you please go home and figure out how to sing so I can have someone to talk to here."

A beep came from the car line, and Raina started to walk off toward a Volkswagen van. Her mom was smoking out the window, giving her a disinterested wave. It didn't look like the nicest greeting.

I thought about Raina walking into the theater earlier. No one had said hi to her. She hadn't smiled at anyone, and no one had smiled at her. In my mind, she was so comfortable with herself, but she didn't look that way right now. She looked a little uncertain, standing there outside her mom's van.

Before she got in, Raina turned back just once.

"You can't just be invisible all the time," she said.

"Why not?" I said.

"Because then the bad guys win."

She got in the backseat of her mom's van, and waved away some cigarette smoke. She slumped back in her seat. And as the van passed by, she didn't look my way again. She was back in her own mind. My mom was nearly up to where I was standing now, but she still couldn't see me.

Maybe I was invisible.

I looked down at my script.

"Well . . . shit," I said.

A week later I was cast as Oliver.

And before you think I pulled off some miraculous audition the way Raina did in New York, let me be clear: There were two very basic reasons for this casting choice, and neither of them had to do with acting or singing. The real reasons were:

1) I hadn't really gone through puberty yet.

And:

2) My singing voice was incredibly high (see Reason 1).

As Raina had predicted, human males were a pretty hot commodity in the world of children's community theater. And the other boys who showed up were both substantially larger than me. One even had stubble. He was obviously cast as Bill Sikes. The other one was kind of weasely looking, so, of course, he was Fagin. The rest of the orphans would be played by girls. Which left me and my glorious (unintentional) falsetto to play Oliver.

There was only one saving grace to the whole disaster, which was that Raina was cast as Nancy. And while I certainly wasn't her love interest, we did have scenes together, and we did engage in many a chaste motherly hug. We even had a song. The aptly named "I'd Do Anything." And it was going to require a lot of practice.

And so it began: the golden era of Raina and Ethan.

For the next month or so, I went over to her house every day after school and danced with her in an unfinished basement while her distracted, arty mom worked on her sculptures in her studio above us.

Prior to this point in time, I had been a strict non-dancer. And as far as I was concerned, singing was reserved for birthdays and the one time a year my family went to church. But in Raina's basement, which was damp and cool and smelled like fabric softener and cat litter, I felt safe enough to hop around like a fool, singing in a bad British accent.

Raina, too, was back in her element, bossing me around like we were on the playground again. "No, no, no, don't turn like that." "Ethan, *stage right*! You're killing me here." She had a bit more patience this time around. It helped that she knew I was bad from the beginning. And since I was at rock bottom, I could only get better. She seemed to take a genuine interest in making me "not horrible," maybe just so her scene wouldn't suck. But maybe, I hoped, because she was starting to care about me.

Rehearsals were the official reason I was at her house, but if it hadn't been for the downtime, I might still have quit. The dancing and singing were an endurance test for the most part, something to get through so we could sit talking on the ugly orange couch in her basement. Usually, we just joked about the scene—trading inappropriate lines in exaggerated accents—but eventually things got a bit more personal. In that last half hour before I headed home to dinner, we talked about anything that was on our minds. Which is how I first heard about Raina's mom.

"Have you ever wondered why she doesn't talk to me?" she said one day.

We were at opposite ends of the orange couch, drinking the juice boxes that Raina's mom still bought for her.

"Who?"

I knew immediately who she was talking about, but I didn't want her to think it was so obvious.

Raina pointed upstairs.

"She talks to you," I said.

"Not really. I mean, she says stuff to me. *Raina, you got your lunch? Is that thing today?* But we don't talk. I can't remember the last time we actually had a conversation about something real. We talked about her and my dad's separation like six months ago maybe, but when I asked her why she married him in the first place, she called me judgmental and went to bed."

"So, what's the deal?" I asked.

I was a little surprised that the conversation had taken this turn. Only minutes before, we had been talking about Mrs. Salazar's stretch pants.

"She's in hibernation," she said.

"Hibernation?"

"Basically, she forgets that other people exist. She just goes in her cave and makes stuff all day and resents everyone who bothers her. She told me once that she probably could have been famous if she didn't have me so young."

"That's kind of harsh."

Raina shrugged.

"I know. You're not supposed to say that to your kid. But she's probably right. She basically gave everything up until I was ten. Then, I guess all her gallery contacts were shot or her work felt old-fashioned. I don't know. Mostly she blames my dad. But he's not here anymore. So, now she blames me."

"And, she just ignores you?"

"When she's in hibernation."

"How long has she been in hibernation?"

"Five years, more or less."

Raina didn't speak for a moment. She took a sip out of her tiny straw.

"I think she hates me, Ethan."

"That can't be true," I said.

Raina got up and listened at the stairs to make sure her mom wasn't in earshot.

"Fine. She loves me. In the way that she has to. She gave birth to me. But if she didn't have to love me that way, she would hate me."

"But I don't . . ."

"Just for being here. That's why. And because I'm young and I have everything in front of me. Maybe that. Or because I look like my dad. Or because I'm kind of a weirdo and a pain in the ass. Could be any or all of that."

She sat back on the couch and stared at the box of juice in her hand. There was a drawing of a dancing apple on the carton, a big smile on its face.

"Either way, my mom doesn't talk to me. And it's really goddamn lonely around here."

From upstairs, we could hear her mom tromping around. She turned up her music, and a classical piano piece hammered through the floorboards.

"I just don't understand," I said.

"Well, that's how it is! I should know," said Raina.

"No," I said. "I totally believe you. I just don't know how anyone could . . ."

"Could what?" she snapped.

"Ignore you."

The low keys of the piano piece thundered above.

"Oh," she said.

I stayed still on my end of the couch. We listened to the end of a piece from a grumpy old composer. Each note sounded like an indictment of life itself.

"Have you ever been to the Green Street Cinema?" I asked.

She shook her head.

"We should go sometime."

"I'm not allowed to go on dates," she said. "My mom doesn't want me making her same mistake."

"Jesus, Nancy," I said in my awful British accent. "Who said it was a date? I'm half your age!"

She smiled.

"It's a weird place," I said. "I just think you might like it."

10

I should have known the Green Street was doomed the day I discovered the Styrofoam beam. It happened last fall when we were doing a "Westerns on Wednesdays" series. I think Randy hoped retirees might show up to watch their childhood heroes act overly masculine in a dusty landscape. Anyway, Lucas and Griffin were tying licorice ropes into lassos and swapping John Wayne quotes like imbeciles.

"I never apologize," shouted Lucas. "It's a sign of weakness!"

He swung his red rope over his head.

"Courage is being scared to death," yelled Griffin, "but saddling up anyway!"

Lucas was making me film all this on his phone. He was always talking about making a movie, but he never showed us anything he'd actually cut together. He just had endless amounts of footage, mostly on his phone, that he never did anything with. He'd come in with pep in his step some days, talking about an epic he was envisioning.

"It's going to be a neo-realist thing," he'd say, "like De Sica, Only about my life. The life of a movie theater worker. Working-class cinema, you know? The plight of an immigrant artist trying to make it in an indifferent capitalist world."

Other days, he'd look totally dejected and when we'd ask him why, he'd say:

"Frank Capra was right. The cardinal sin of filmmaking is dullness." Then, he'd sulk off to replace the hand soap in the restrooms.

The day I found the beam, he was aiming a licorice lasso at Griffin's head. I didn't have the heart to ask him how this fit in with his movie. But I was filming it dutifully.

"If you've got 'em by the balls," he said, "their hearts and minds will follow. Hiya, Cowpoke!"

He let go of his rope and it soared over Griffin's head and hit a wooden beam on the ceiling. I followed the flight of the rope with the camera, and so I saw clearly that instead of slamming against the beam and falling back down, there was an explosion of white dust, and the entire beam wobbled and dropped down where it landed, without much sound at all.

"Oh shit," said Griffin, speaking for all of us.

We all walked over to the fallen beam. There was a healthy chunk missing from it, and inside was pure Styrofoam. The whole beam was painted to look like wood. It was a decorative beam.

"That can't be good," said Lucas.

He motioned for me to turn off the camera.

"Styrofoam is really terrible for the environment," said Griffin.

We all agreed that this was true. And that the best thing to do was to get on a ladder, put it back, and pretend we had never seen just how fragile the bones of our temple really were.

I was staring up at this secret beam when Sweet Lou stepped out of the ladies' restroom and walked past me. Her dyed red bangs hung over her eyes, and her cane dug into the carpet with each stride. She put a hand to her head and looked out into the fading sunlight then she croaked over her shoulder.

"That asshole's back."

And before I had time to respond, she was gone. When I faced the door, there was the squinty man again, outside with a bunch of other men in matching gray suits. He was gesticulating and pointing wildly at things in the neighborhood. A few regular customers had to dodge the group to find their way inside the building for the evening film. At one point, squinty man himself was actually blocking the door.

"Ugh. Ron Marsh," came a voice from behind me.

I turned around and found Griffin refilling the soda machine with Coke syrup. More than a couple of times in my tenure as manager, I'd caught him syphoning off the syrup into a cup and drinking it straight, which I don't recommend. It tastes a little like how I imagine sugar would taste if someone scraped the skin off your tongue right before you ate a spoonful.

"What did you say?" I said.

"Ron Marsh," he pointed outside. "I can't stand that dude."

"How do you know his name?"

He blinked.

"Oh, I went to his office, yesterday."

I nearly fell over.

"What?"

"Yeah, I was going to give him a piece of my mind, but then when I showed up, the secretary was really nice to me, and he wasn't around. I didn't think it would be fair to yell at her just because she works for a dildo, so I just came back here."

Outside, Ron Marsh was laughing at what appeared to be his own joke. The men in suits were also laughing. Griffin watched them.

"I'm sorry, Griffin. What are you saying?"

"Nothing really. The whole thing was kind of a waste of time if you want the honest truth. But yeah, anyway, his name is Ron Marsh and he has a pretty fancy office. There were M&Ms with his initials on them in the waiting room. I ate a green one. It was delicious."

We both looked out at Ron again.

"Well, he's standing out there right now," I said. "If you want to go tackle him or something."

"No thanks," he said. "I think my natural state might be pacifism. An eye for an eye will only make the whole world blind, you know?"

"Uh-huh," I said.

"Gandhi said that."

I started walking toward the door, picking up speed as I went.

"*Mahatma* Gandhi," he said.

"I know who Gandhi is!" I said.

I swung the door open, and it breezed right past the back of Ron Marsh's head, sending his hair straight up in a gust of man-made wind. The group of men in suits took a step back. Ron wheeled around and frowned.

"Can I help you with something, Wendy?" he asked.

I stood looking at him for a moment. Whatever sense of righteous indignation had sent me out there was already wearing off.

"Yes, Ron Marsh," I said slowly. "As a matter of fact you

can. You are blocking the main entrance to my theater, making it difficult for my customers to come inside and watch awesome movies. . . ."

"*Your* theater?" he said.

I just stared back at him. He did not back down.

"Did you just say this was *your* theater?"

"Well," I said. "I mean . . ."

"Oh, no. I'm afraid this is not your theater, Wendy," he said. "It is the university's theater. Randy Frick was renting it for a while, but he forfeited that privilege when he stopped paying his bills. And the only reason it's still open as we speak is because of the capital market."

"The capital market?" I said. The words tasted unfamiliar in my mouth.

There were a few nods from the suits. Ron exhaled.

"Eventually, you'll come to realize that there are bigger forces in the world than what you want. In this case, capital. The market wasn't so great the last few years, so the university took our foot off the gas pedal when it comes to real estate projects. But now the market's back! So, here we are."

He winked at the guy next to him.

"Anyway, this theater, no matter who is running it, is a blight on the neighborhood and the campus. You have to know this! Look at it! No one uses it. And it's already falling apart. I'm sorry that this situation will no longer allow you to make minimum wage while you crack smug jokes with your friends. But that's the way it goes."

"A dollar more," I said.

"I'm sorry . . ."

"I make a dollar more than minimum wage," I said. "Because I make the schedule. And order the films. And restock the snacks. And I make sure the seats aren't sticky. I clean them myself. So that when someone comes here to leave the world of capital markets behind, they can watch something strange in a clean seat."

Ron Marsh was staring at me. The suits were staring at me.

"If you'll excuse me . . ." he said.

Ron was turning his back on me when the door opened and I heard a familiar smoker's rasp:

"So, you boys are good with the Historic Preservation Commission, then?"

Sweet Lou stood in the doorway, a cigarette already burning in her thin lips.

"I'm sorry. Who are you?" Ron asked.

Lou waved away his question.

"Before you all get too excited about making your shiny new building, you should know that a nomination has been filed in favor of putting this building on the National Registry. It was built by Liebenberger and Katz."

There were blank looks all around.

"Liebenberger?" Ron said eventually.

"And Katz," said Sweet Lou. "Don't forget about Katz. Real famous. They built theaters all around the country. Most people think Liebenberger was the genius since he was the more famous of the two. But Katz was amazing with acoustics. A real visionary."

Ron, for the first time, seemed at a total loss for words.

"One thing you boys will have to realize," said Lou, "is that sometimes there are bigger forces in the world than what you want."

She coughed and sent her cigarette rocketing over their heads. They watched it whizzing past, and I saw a few men flinch when it hit the ground in an eruption of sparks. Then, Lou held the door open for me and waved me inside. I looked at Ron, desperately trying to think of a stinging parting phrase.

"Yeah, Ron!" I said.

It was the best I could come up with.

Then I walked inside the Green Street and watched all the fancy men stand there another moment before Ron turned and led them down the street. Behind me, Lou was leaning against the concessions counter, chuckling to herself. She pulled a wad of napkins out of the dispenser and wiped her perspiring forehead.

"Whoa, Lou," I said. "That was kind of amazing. I had

no idea about the preservation commission. How did you know all that stuff about the architects?"

She leaned on her cane and watched the lights of the marquee come to life outside. Her brow folded over her narrow eyes.

"Are you kidding me?" she said. "I have no idea who built this place."

I could feel my smile freezing.

"What do you mean?" I said. "What about Liebenberger and . . ."

"Katz. Those were my boyfriends from Hebrew camp."

She grimaced and cleared some phlegm from her throat. I knew it was time to stop asking questions, but I couldn't help myself.

"So, you haven't really filed a . . . nomination?"

"God no," she said. "This place is about to collapse. But *they* don't know that, do they? Just because an old lady says it, it must be true! It should buy us a little more time, at least."

Lou released a cough then that sounded like a small pipe bomb going off. And it occurred to me that maybe "a little more time" was all she cared about. She was getting up there, and if she put off the demise of this place a little longer, that might be enough. Me on the other hand: I was hoping for something a little longer term. Lou stepped over and put a hand on my shoulder.

"Sorry I don't have the answer, kid. But, you know, maybe you shouldn't be putting all your eggs in this basket anyway."

I looked at Lou's callused hand.

"I don't have any other baskets," I said.

She stifled another cough and looked me in the eye.

"You're young. You seem healthy. You're less of an idiot than most. Tell me: There really isn't anything else you care about?"

SUBJECTIVE SOUND

A sound used to show the interior state of the character.

Example: In *The Godfather*, when Michael goes into the bathroom to grab the gun that's behind the toilet, he hears trains that are so loud they block out the other sounds. But the restaurant isn't near train tracks. He's hearing them in his head because he's about to kill someone.

I wish I heard trains. There's something almost romantic about that. Instead, when I'm really nervous (say about seeing someone I haven't seen in a long time) I just hear this low-level buzz, like a chorus of cicadas singing in my brain.

I have to listen for it, but it's always there. It's my subjective sound.

11

When I got to her house, I didn't recognize her.

I walked up the chipped brick sidewalk, all the way to the front porch, and I didn't know it was Raina. She wasn't facing me, so at least I'm not that oblivious. She was standing on top of an old blue cooler, holding a large plastic bag of some kind. Her blond hair was mostly gone; that was part of the problem. From the back, she looked like a ten-year-old boy. And she was even skinnier than I remembered. But when she turned around, spilling birdseed on my shoes in the process, her familiar half smile brought her lovely face back to life.

"I read online that if you feed the birds," she said, "you have to do it consistently."

She stepped down from the cooler, letting the bag of seed thump to the ground.

"If they get used to a neighborhood feeder and then you

take it away, they might just all die off. They come to rely on it, you know?"

She looked up at the feeder suctioned to the window. It was overflowing with seed now, but, so far, there were no takers.

"I've been gone awhile, though," she said, "and the renters never filled it up. Which means I probably single-handedly killed off every bird in this place."

She scanned the neighborhood, as if she might still be able to see their corpses littering the streets and yards around us. She looked genuinely concerned.

"I haven't heard about any bird pandemics around here," I said. "I think you're in the clear."

If she heard me, she didn't respond.

"Besides," I said. "Have you ever seen Hitchcock's *The Birds*? Those little bastards are just waiting to turn on us."

She opened the screen door. I hesitated a moment, but then I stepped inside. I noticed a difference in the place immediately. All their furniture was the same, but it had been rearranged, and whoever the renters were, they hadn't exactly been kind to the place. There were little holes in the walls from poorly hung pictures. The carpet was worn, and the couch by the TV was missing a cushion. Raina watched me take the place in.

"Mom's not happy to be back. The place in California has a pool."

The classical music was there again, booming through the ceiling.

"What about you?" I said.

She shrugged.

"I never learned to swim," she said.

We kept walking into the kitchen, and then, as if we'd never skipped a beat, we headed down the stairs to the basement where we used to rehearse after school. I was relieved to see that this space was largely unchanged. The ugly orange couch was still ugly and orange, and the room still smelled like fresh laundry. Raina took a seat on the couch, and I stayed standing nearby.

Suddenly, the room felt a whole lot smaller to me, like it had shrunk in the time Raina was away. Obviously, we were just bigger, but anything seemed possible in that moment. Maybe the walls were slowly closing in. Raina looked me over, and as if she'd read my mind, she said:

"You got tall."

It was true, I guess. I had grown a lot in the last few years, and most of it vertically. I had to duck my head to get under the low doorframe in our upstairs bathroom. And Mom always asked me to get her food processor down from the high cabinets when she was making pesto.

"It's all an illusion," I said. "These are five-inch heels."

"Ah," she said. "That must be it."

In the brief, awkward silence that followed, I heard the

dehumidifier switch on and fill the gap with its watery drone.

"You got skinny," I said.

Her smile disappeared. I closed my mouth. I hadn't meant it to come out so bluntly. I hadn't meant to say anything at all. I opened my mouth again:

"I mean, it's not—"

"You don't have to backpedal," she said. "I get it. I *am* skinny. I was seeing this nutritionist my manager recommended, and she put me on a macrobiotic diet."

"A what?"

Raina looked down.

"No. Seriously," I said. "I don't know what that means."

"It means no wheat. No eggs. No meat or dairy."

"Holy shit. What's left?"

"I was encouraged to eat sea vegetables."

"Sea vegetables?"

"You know, brown kelp, sea lettuce. My mom got really into algae. She ate that shit like it was pudding."

I had to concentrate to keep from gagging.

"I don't know what to say. I always thought algae was just like pond scum."

"You're not far off. I wasn't supposed to lose so much weight; I was just supposed to be detoxing. But I guess I went a little overboard."

"Is that why you were crying in Dairy Queen?"

"Part of it," she said.

I wasn't sure what to do with my hands, just standing there. I clasped them behind my back, but that felt weird, too. I hunched a little, making myself smaller.

"Will you sit down?" she said. "You're making me super nervous."

I kept standing. I thought about moving toward the couch, but my feet weren't really into that plan. I noticed I was bouncing a little in place, but I couldn't seem to make that stop, either.

"I should probably go," I said suddenly.

Raina looked shocked.

"You just got here."

I pulled out my phone and checked the time.

"I have to get to work."

"It's been literally five minutes. That's not a real visit, Ethan."

The truth was I had another hour at least until I had to work. Lucas was opening and there wasn't a film until three o'clock. But now that I had said I had to go, I couldn't take it back. Raina looked deflated, like all of her suspicions had been confirmed. Her eyes darted around the room, looking for someplace to land.

I wanted to take it back, but Raina spoke before I could: "Your mom said you're basically managing the place now."

"It just kind of happened," I said.

"She told my mom that you're there all the time. Like you barely even come home anymore."

"I come home," I said. "But I am there a lot. I don't know. I guess it's just where I want to be."

It took all of my meager reserves of restraint not to tell her the whole sob story about the eviction. Or the real reasons I stayed there so much. How I actually didn't feel good anywhere else, including my own house, which felt like it had been remodeled while I wasn't there. But I couldn't get into it for some reason. Maybe I thought I would cry. Or maybe it was because I was angry that she had never made her absence right. In short: I was feeling too many things. And my ears were buzzing.

I was quiet for a few seconds. Then I realized I was waiting for her to tell me what to do the way she always had. Despite everything that had happened, if she had told me to stay, just given me a simple command—"Sit down and stay here, Ethan"—I would have done it. But it was like her macrobiotic diet had taken away both her dairy and her fire. I turned toward the door.

"Do you still remember the dance?" she asked suddenly.

I looked at her on the couch. She didn't move.

"You mean . . ."

"Our dance. From the play."

"I don't think so," I said. "It's been too long. I'm not sure I ever knew it."

She looked at me for a long time before she finally blinked.

"Yeah," she said. "Stupid question."

I was sweating now, despite the cool of the basement.

"You never told me how it went," she said.

"How what went?"

"Your scene. With that girl who took my place."

Again, I thought about telling her the truth. The dehumidifier switched off, leaving us in humidified silence.

"Oh, it went great," I said. "We brought down the house."

12

This, of course, was a lie.

Zero houses were brought down. Zero greatness achieved.

It wasn't my proudest moment. I'd told myself I would stick with theater even if Raina never came back from New York. I had actually tried something new, and it felt cowardly to give it up just because she was gone. I had to suck it up. Stay strong. Etcetera. So, I resolved to dance with another Nancy. To bow and turn and do the fox-trot while singing in an absurd cockney falsetto. And when I went back to the Playhouse that Saturday, Mrs. Salazar took me aside and introduced me to my new scene partner.

Her name was Vanessa Drake and she was what my grandmother would call "a nice young lady." She was freckled and fair-skinned, and when we shook hands her palm was sweaty. She had a retainer and when she was nervous she launched it out of her mouth and chewed on it for a second before clicking it back into place with the tip of her tongue. I could tell she was amped to play Nancy. She'd been plucked from the chorus and given a lead, and she wasn't even pretending to be sad that Raina was gone.

"My mom says it's irresponsible parenting," she said, while we waited for our instructions. "Letting her do all that movie stuff. She's not even eighteen."

"Uh-huh," I said, trying not to think too much about Raina.

Vanessa Drake, I'm sure, had her doubts about me as a partner. As she should have. I didn't exactly carry myself like a leading man. And I was a newbie through and through. But when Mrs. Salazar had us try out the scene, I was shocked to find that I had actually made some progress. Every dorky pirouette, every little doff of my cap was on point. That damn routine was imprinted in my brain. The only difference was the level of passion. With Raina, I had been singing with every fiber of my soul. This time the words rang hollow.

"I'd do anything. For you, dear, anything. For you mean everything to me."

I was on key, but, alas, there was no song in my heart. I led Vanessa Drake across the dusty theater stage and then stopped to jump and click my heels.

"I know that I'd go anywhere. For your smile, anywhere, for your smile, everywhere, I'd see."

Raina had been gone for two weeks, and I already knew she wouldn't be coming back to Minnesota. Why would she? It was only a matter of time until someone else figured out what I had known for years: Raina Allen was supposed to be famous. And now that she'd been noticed, she was going to ascend to her rightful throne, and those of us who were lucky to know her way back when would become the charming hometown friends she thought fondly of from time to time. In other words, I was no longer a lead in her life. I was an extra.

I tried to shove all this out of my mind as I danced with Vanessa. I tried to imagine that I was back in Raina's basement. That I'd be sipping a juice box any minute, laughing about the guys at my school who were trying to grow mustaches in the eighth grade. I tried to pretend that my heart was not slowly dissolving into a toxic puddle that would never quite reconstitute. In other words, I tried acting.

But as Vanessa started in on her part of the song, it wasn't quite taking.

"Would you lace my shoe?"

She thrust her immaculate white sneaker into the air.

"Anything," I said in a monotone.

"Paint your face bright blue?"

"Anything."

This one barely above a whisper.

Mrs. Salazar who had mostly been watching me in a

stupefied state of wonder so far, now yelled from the foot of the stage.

"A little more enthusiasm on those *anythings*, Ethan!"

"Catch a kangeroo?"

"No," I said.

Vanessa's retainer smile dimmed. But she took my improvisation in stride.

"Go to Timbuktu?"

I stopped dancing altogether.

"No, I wouldn't," I said. "I wouldn't go to goddamn Timbuktu. Why would I do that?"

Gradually Vanessa came to a stop. She looked at Mrs. Salazar, and then back at me.

"Ethan," said Mrs. Salazar, "that was going so well. Are you okay?"

"No," I said again. "I'm not okay."

She was about to ask a follow-up question, but I wasn't done.

"I'm just telling the truth. I wouldn't do those things. What's the point?"

"What are you even talking about?" asked poor Vanessa, chewing the wire of her retainer. "It's just a song."

I barely heard her.

"I think I'm just going to lie down here if nobody minds."

They stared at me as I lay down, and rested my heavy head on the stage.

"Uh, Ethan," said Mrs. Salazar, "this is very odd. Do I need to phone your mother?"

I looked at the stage lights above me. They were buzzing in the quiet of the small auditorium. I was already seeing blue spots at the corners of my vision. I wondered if this was what doing a death scene was like. I could see the appeal of that kind of acting. How amazing would it be to come out on stage and die every night, only to be reborn in the next performance?"

"He's not moving," said Vanessa.

She was standing over me now, examining my face with no discernible pity. I could kind of see up her skirt. Her underwear was blue.

"Is he conscious?" asked Mrs. Salazar.

"Yes!" she yelled. "He's conscious. But I think he's crying. Ethan, are you crying?"

Ethan's Glossary of Film Terms

ENTRY #99

TEAR STICK

This is a wax tube that looks like lipstick.
It has menthol and camphor and if you put
a small amount in your eye, it creates real
tears.

Actors use it to cry if they can't cry for
real.

I have never needed a tear stick.

13

Whoever came up with the rule that men can't cry was a real dick-bat in my opinion. I guess maybe it was valuable to be stoic back when we had to keep feral warthogs from running off with our children. But seriously, we're not supposed to cry when life is frustrating and tragic? Our forefathers were idiots. Emotionally stunted idiots. And I intend to dishonor their legacy with my salty man tears.

I do most of my crying in my car. It's a good place for it, I find.

It doesn't take me very long either. I just kind of sit there and let the tears stream down my face. Then I wipe my nose on my sleeve (like a man) and get on with my day. Going to see Raina brought a lot of emotions back, I guess. The dual abandonment of her leaving and my father dying. And the way she looked, all thin and defeated.

I didn't know what to do or say, so I left like a weakling.

Leaving: that was the weak part. Not the crying.

When I finished, I walked around to the back of the Green Street, where we share a couple Dumpsters with the corporate Noodle place next door. I'm not sure why I went back there. Maybe I didn't want to walk in the front door with a runny nose and puffy cheeks, even though Lucas probably wasn't here yet. Or maybe I was nostalgic for the smell of baking trash. But I just stood there for a moment looking around the alley at the backs of all the old buildings in our row.

The view was even worse than the front. A mess of tangled electrical cords and rusted gutters. Chipped brick and touch-up paint that didn't match the original coat. The theater wasn't open yet, so there was no sign of civilization. Just me: a lanky dude in an alley. Well, just a lanky dude in an alley, and the Oracle, watching me out of the sole window of the projection room. I heard a tapping on the glass, and when I looked up, there she was, shrouded in darkness. She cracked the window.

"Afternoon, boss," she said.

She looked around the alley, just as I had. If she thought much about the view, she didn't say. She just blinked through her glasses and then spoke again.

"What do you know about a man named Henri Langlois?"

She pronounced the name in a very French-sounding way.

"I'm not really sure what you just said," I answered.

She nodded. It was hard knowing everything. She dropped something down to me. It fluttered through the air and landed at my feet. It was a five-dollar bill folded into an origami crane. I picked it up and cupped it in my palm.

"I don't think this will cover our debt," I said.

"I'm out of Almond Milk," said Anjo. "Go pick some up at the co-op and we'll talk."

I unfolded the crane and turned it back into money, the root of all our problems. I looked up once again to find Anjo, but she was gone.

I returned with the milk about fifteen minutes later, and found her threading the projector for the first show of the day. She moved across the room with purpose, pulling the film from one part of the oversized projector to the next, lacing it over the sprockets and through the gates. It was like watching a dance: you knew it had been practiced a thousand times, but it looked so effortless in front of you. While she threaded, she began the story of that French guy she spoke about.

"Henri Langlois," she said, "was the director of the Cinémathèque Française. Ring a bell?"

I shook my head. She clucked her tongue.

"And you call yourself a cinephile."

"Do I call myself that?"

"It was a film organization," she said. "And it had a small, sixty-seat movie theater in Paris. Mr. Langlois was the manager, like you."

She breezed by me and winked.

"But he wasn't just an ordinary theater manager," she added. "He was a revolutionary!"

She let that sink in a moment.

"How?" I asked.

"He dedicated his life to preserving movies, and he kept his theater running during the Nazi Occupation of Paris. He saved films from being destroyed, hiding them in his bathtub until they could be screened again. And after the war, his theater became one of the most famous in the world. It's where the French New Wave was born."

She made some adjustments to the projector, switching it on to advance the film. My breath came easier. Seeing Anjo work made the whole universe feel like it was in order. Like she was secretly the one setting the whole thing in motion.

"Okay," I said, looking away. "This French guy was a hero. And I don't mean to be selfish, but how is that supposed to help us?"

"I'm not done yet," she said.

Satisfied with her work, Anjo walked over to her little fridge and poured herself a bowl of flaxy granola. She went heavy on the almond milk.

"The plot thickens," she said, "when the French government thinks Langlois's movie collection has become too valuable to be managed by the famous curmudgeon. In 1968, after fighting over the direction of the theater for years, they fired Langlois and changed the locks on his building."

"Damn," I said. "What happened to him?"

"Within the span of a single day, filmmakers from across the globe withdrew the rights to have their films shown at the Cinémathèque Française. Charlie Chaplin. Orson Welles. Half a week later, three thousand people showed up to protest and were beaten by the police. Truffaut was wounded!"

She took a teeming mouthful of granola, and smiled through her bite.

"Meanwhile, the list of artists protesting the firing kept growing. Pablo Picasso signed a petition. Alfred Hitchcock. Demonstrations kept forming. Police violence continued. The boy who played the lead in the 400 *Blows* gave a speech at one rally. Finally, months later, the government surrendered. Langlois was reinstated. His funding was cut, but he had won back his kingdom."

She set her bowl of granola down and fired up the projector.

"Later that year, there were massive protests against the government. Some people think the desire to save Langlois started it all. A cultural revolution began with a fight for movies. In a theater smaller than this one."

She motioned me toward the opening to the theater. I got up and stood next to her. Down below, an image leaped onto the screen. It was a black-and-white shot of a crowd making a run against police in riot gear. French teenagers kicked at the shields and put their arms up to keep the truncheons from landing on their heads. Flyers denouncing the government rained down over the heads of the protesters. The sound of sirens echoed through the streets.

"Can you imagine it?" she said. "People fighting the police to save the movie theater they loved. To save their right to watch the movies from Langlois's bathtub."

I looked next to me at Anjo. Her expression was solemn. She reached out and turned my head back to the screen. In the foreground of the shot now was a gangly guy with a nest of dark hair, holding his arms up in the air and screaming his lungs out. He was wild with revolt, defending what he believed in.

But he didn't look like a revolutionary. His was not an imposing physical presence. His skinny arms flailed in the night. He looked like the last guy to get picked in gym class. But here he was actually doing something, putting his body on the line. He looked like a man who had discovered what he really cared about.

He looked, on closer inspection, kind of like me.

14

I t's probably about time I introduced the regulars.

Because as much as I was heartbroken about everything going on, they were going to be affected by all of this, too, though they didn't know it yet. They were relatively few, the regulars, but they made for a memorable bunch. And they broke down into a handful of recognizable categories. So, if you'll permit me a quick break, here's a who's who of the people who actually paid to come to the Green Street.

First, may I present:

The Collectors. These are the people who seek the unseen gems and rarities of the cinema because they need to complete their personal filmography. Like bird-watchers crossing a red-throated loon from their life list, they come to the Green Street for a rare film sighting in the wild. Whether it's a showing of an obscure horror movie like *Rats: Night of Terror* (which is a real movie and comes highly recommended), or a rare pristine print of *Pather Panchali* by Satyajit Ray they come simply to check it off their list. A list, lucky for us, that can never be completed in one lifetime.

Next we have:

The College Hepcats (do I have to say hipster?). I'll admit right away, I am less fond of this group. You know them by now. Those glasses. Those sneakers. Those loud, often wrong opinions. I really want to give them the benefit of the doubt. They're trying to like interesting things. They're making an effort. But do the guys always have to bring a girl that they're trying to impress? Do they have to mumble a running commentary in her ear during the entire film? Do they have to bring their own bags of lightly salted pistachios and crunch them at maximum volume? The answer, of course, is yes. They have to do all these things or else you might mistake them for an average person just trying to live life and be happy: their worst nightmare.

Oh, and speaking of nightmares, next are:

The High-Art Perverts. They claim to be here for the art, but they only seem to show up to French films with prostitutes and prominent three-way sex scenes. They always sit in the back; they never buy snacks. And sometimes, when they're acting particularly bold, they'll ask for the movie poster on the way out. "I became a bit smitten with the leading lady in that one!" I heard once. And though I wanted to say "Sir, I am not going to give you a vintage *Vivre Sa Vie* poster so you can go home and make it your new girlfriend," I couldn't say anything, though because you can't kick someone out just for asking about a poster. I keep my eye on them, though. Even when I didn't want to.

And lastly, we have:

The Escapists. The ones who can only feel emotions when they're watching a movie. Lucky for us, they like classics, so they come to repertory theaters like ours when we're showing old stuff. They're the ones who cry like babies at the end of *The Bicycle Thief*, and come out of *Bringing Up Baby* completely renewed in their own absurd search for love. They come here to feel every emotion that is probably missing from their lonely, daily lives. You can recognize them by the profound changes they go through from the time they enter the theater and the time they leave. And, of course, they always come alone.

Guess who's a member of that category?

I'm not just a member; I am their president.

And there you have it. The basic roster of our patrons. How many were they total? Fifty? A hundred if you turned on all the lights and watched them scatter? We complained about them to be sure. They were odd ducks. Out of step with the world outside. But they were also extended family, so we cut them some slack. And, most importantly, they had all chosen the Green Street as their place.

Just like us.

Outside of this theater, they probably never would have crossed paths. The only thing that united them was their strange loyalty to this building and the flickering lights within. And as you might have guessed already, I was quickly hatching a plan to put that loyalty to the test.

"I don't understand," said Lucas. "Where would we even march?"

"I've mapped out a route," I said, pointing to the back of my flyer. "We walk down Green Street, through the quad, and eventually to the president's office, where we stay until our demands are heard. We may or may not have to chain ourselves to his door and urinate in a bucket."

In front of me on the counter of the concession stand was a stack of freshly copied flyers that read, "SAVE THE GREEN STREET!" Then below there was a date and time and a sign-off, "VANQUISH THE PROFITEERS!"

"Are we really going to vanquish anyone?" asked Griffin. "That seems kind of harsh."

"You cannot make a revolution with silk gloves," said Lucas.

"Who said that?" asked Griffin, "Was it Gandhi?"

"Joseph Stalin," said Lucas.

Griffin took this in. He jammed his hand into an enormous bag of "Flavor-blasted" Goldfish crackers, and stuffed a few in his mouth.

"It has to be a peaceful protest," he said, mouth full. "Or it won't fit my new ethos."

"I don't remember your *new ethos* kicking in yesterday when you laughed at that shark movie where the guy got ripped in half. How many times did you make me re-watch that?"

Griffin stuffed more fish in his mouth.

"That was fake," he said. "At least I'm pretty sure it was. Was that fake?"

"Relax, guys," I said. "It will be metaphorical vanquishing. As much as I feel like launching Molotov cocktails, I'm not sure that's going to get much done except put us on some kind of university watch list. We need people on our side. And some positive media attention wouldn't hurt."

"Jesus, Wendy," said Griffin. "Listen to you. You're like Sean Penn from *Milk*, or Denzel Washington from *Cry Freedom*."

"Do you know any actual activists? Not just the actors that played them?"

"I'm gonna need one of those scooters," came a croak from behind us.

Lucas startled.

"Jesus, Lou, you can't sneak up on us like that!" he said.

Lou asserted herself into our circle.

"I'm just sayin'," she said. "Realistically, I can't really

walk your whole route. But if you want me there, I'm gonna need some transportation. Probably a Rascal."

Griffin crunched a Goldfish, lost in thought.

"Rascals are superexpensive, even with an insurance rebate," he said.

"How do you know that?" asked Lucas.

"My aunt has a mobility scooter. It took her two years to pay that thing off."

Sweet Lou just watched him for a moment. It was hard to tell if she was incredulous or just zoning out.

"Maybe you should sit this one out, Lou," I said. "What if things get ugly? I saw these French kids . . ."

"That's exactly why you need me!" she shouted. "If the campus police want to tango, they'll have to go through an old lady. Plus I was protesting when you guys were still wetting the bed."

"Griffin still wets the bed," said Lucas.

Lou put an unlit cigarette between her lips. Then she made her way toward the door.

"I need some wheels, boys," she said. "Deliver and I'll ride beside you."

ETHAN'S GLOSSARY OF FILM TERMS

ENTRY #83

MODESTY PASTIES

The flimsy little coverings that actors wear
during sex scenes.

They're supposed to keep actual body parts
from showing or touching, but apparently, they
always fall off.

Lucas has made a game of spotting them in
movies, and he's been known to shout them
out in the middle of a scene.

"Tan thong!" he yelled once during a European
film. "Tan thong!"

Once you start looking, it's not hard to
find them. I've always found them reassuring
somehow. A little reminder that movies aren't
real no matter how much you want them to be.
And that people's genitals aren't touching.

15

At home that night, I holed up in my room and watched a movie called *The Dreamers* by Bernardo Bertolucci. While I watched, I stuffed envelopes full of flyers. Anjo had told me to watch the film for inspiration. It's where she had gotten the documentary footage of the rioting teens. And sure enough, early in the movie our American hero meets an alluring French brother and sister at the Cinémathèque Française. They flee the protests together. From there, however, it pretty much turns into a High Art Pervert film, which I didn't entirely mind (movie sex is, obviously, the only sex in my life). Except when my mom walked in the middle of the most graphic scene.

I tried to hit stop, but instead I hit pause right as our hero's butt cheeks were flexed in extreme close-up. My mother, however, did not look at the television when she came in. She looked at me and the envelopes scattered across my bed. I had been working from an outdated list of "Friends of the Green Street," that I found in Randy's office, and there were probably forty poorly folded flyers surrounding me like paper boats on an ocean of unwashed sheets.

"Ethan," she said, "you've been in here for hours. Your dinner is beyond cold. What are you doing?"

I looked at the large buttocks on the television. Then I looked at the flyers and envelopes spilling over the edge of the bed and onto the floor.

"Well," I said. "It's simple, really."

There had to be another sentence in my head somewhere. I looked at the doorway. Improbably, Mom still hadn't glanced at the television. How was that possible?

"I'm doing some donor outreach."

Her face did not change.

"You know, outreaching to various donors . . ."

Ordinarily, she would have eaten this silly lie alive, but she seemed distracted tonight. She nodded, and swept her blond bangs out of her eyes. She pointed to a corner of my room.

"Those study guides are gathering dust."

Truthfully, I had forgotten all about the guides until she pointed them out. I hadn't read them before I bombed the SATs and I hadn't read them after I bombed the SATs. According to a pact I'd made, I was supposed to be retaking the tests sometime in the indeterminate future. Mom was right, though. The pile of guides was indeed covered in a thick film of particulate matter.

"What if I want to show movies for the rest of my life? Where's the standardized test for that?"

"You're barely being paid," she said, which, unfortunately, was true. I hadn't cut myself a check in weeks.

"Mom," I said. "Do you know who Henri Langlois was?"

I butchered the French pronunciation, but I'm not sure it mattered. She sighed. I could smell the dinner she'd cooked through the door now. Something with a lot of cumin. Probably her Moroccan stew, which I had grown to love after I realized food could actually have spice and flavor. A tough sell in the Midwest.

"You wanted to be a lawyer," she said out of nowhere.

"What?" I laughed. "No I didn't."

She shook her head.

"When you were ten, your father showed you *Inherit the Wind*, that movie about the Scopes trial, and you wanted to be a defense attorney just like Spencer Tracy's character. You walked around the living room for weeks holding us in contempt of court."

"I was just acting out the movie. I did that all the time. Remember my pirate phase? I wore your eyeliner every day for a month."

She wasn't really listening to me now.

"Your junior high science teacher, Mrs. Geyer, said you were the best student she ever had. She said your lab reports were immaculate. That's the word she used. Immaculate."

"Mom, that woman only liked me because I didn't use the Bunsen burners for lighting joints like Aaron Jorgenson."

"You can deny it all you want," said Mom, "but ever since you were a kid, we always heard the same thing. Ethan is so bright. Ethan is so curious. Ethan is going places. And that doesn't mean you need to be a Nobel winner, but I can't believe it's intellectually satisfying for you to shovel popcorn and watch the same movies over and over again in that sad place."

"We're showing art," I said. "These films are major contributions to the human experience!"

"I see," she said. "Could you tell me what exactly the giant ass on your television is contributing to the human experience?"

I felt myself blushing. I picked up the remote and hit stop, and the butt went away.

"Granted," I said. "This isn't Bertolucci's finest film, but . . ."

"Look, Ethan," she said, "you needed time. We both did. I gave you some time. And the truth is I can't force you to do anything anymore. But I want you to think about why you're really spending so much time in that place, and ask yourself if it's really healthy."

I felt the pulse of anger before I could control it.

"At least I'm not lying to myself," I said.

My mom had been calm so far, but now I could see her cheeks getting red.

"I'm sorry," she said. "What?"

I sat up straighter on the bed.

"It's great that you've managed to reinvent your life," I said. "But it's not the same as it was. You know it's not. And you can't cook and knit your way past it all. You think you've moved on, but you've just come up with a bunch of ways to ignore everything. Well, guess what? So have I. I do the things that make me happy, and I'm sorry they don't meet your approval. But why don't you ask yourself why me hanging around the Green Street makes you so uncomfortable. Is it really because I'm underachieving? Or is it because it makes you think about Dad?"

She just stood there for a moment, taking it all in. When she spoke again, it sounded like she was on the verge of tears.

"Well, this has been pleasant," she said. "But I have to go now."

"Where?" I asked.

"I have a date," she said.

I stared at her. It had been a long time since she'd been

on a date, at least that I knew about. I was starting to think she had given up on that part of her life.

"Who is he?" I asked.

My voice was soft, but I know she heard me. She looked up at the ceiling and then back down again.

"Internet guy," she said.

I nodded.

"It's still hard," she said. "Of course it is, Ethan. God-damnit. Do you really think he doesn't cross my mind every day?"

I wanted to respond to this, but she started speaking again.

"But I knew your dad pretty well, and he wouldn't want us to just stay frozen in time. He never stayed still a moment in his life. If he were here, he'd be the one telling us to get off our asses and do something."

"What would he think of Internet guy?" I asked.

I regretted it the instant I said it, but I said it nonetheless.

"Really?" she said. "That's the way it's going to be?"

"I'm sorry," I said. "I . . ."

She just looked at me for a moment then she shut the door and left me alone in my silent bedroom. I looked at all the flyers around me, some folded, some not. The envelopes were addressed to all the regulars I could find, some of whom I'm not sure were still living. I had no idea if any of them would care enough to join us in our march. It didn't seem promising.

I knew Mom had a point about the Green Street. It wasn't just my enthusiasm for movies that was keeping me there. It was a refuge. There was no secret about that. But safe havens were hard to find in life. You could search for years to find a place where your thoughts didn't race. A place that just felt right to you. Why was it such a bad thing to cling to your port when you found it?

I got up from the bed, sending an avalanche of flyers spilling to the floor. I walked over to my closet and pulled out a box from beneath a heap of clothes that no longer fit me, now that I was almost six feet tall. The box was sealed with packing tape, and I used my key to the Green Street to slice through it. The fibers of the packing tape split apart and the flaps popped open. Right on top was one of Dad's books. The cover had a picture of Robert De Niro from *Raging Bull*, shadowboxing in the fog. And above his head, was the title I remembered so clearly:

The Cinema of Revolt.

16

Dad had pretty eclectic taste for a film studies professor. He could talk about the Czech New Wave in the same sentence as *The Fast and the Furious*. And sometimes, I suspected he actually preferred watching terrible action movies on cable to anything else. I never saw Dad happier than stretched out on our old green velour sofa, grinning while Chuck Norris jump kicked somebody off a dusty cliff. But the movies he liked best of all were the ones he'd studied with his mentor in graduate school, the films of the late sixties to the very beginning of the eighties. His first book was about this period, and it was the book I held in my hands now.

He was writing it when I was born. Literally. Mom said he brought a notebook into the delivery room and scrawled like a madman while she labored for ten hours. He felt the impending doom of his free time, and he knew he needed to finish it if he wanted a teaching job to support his new family. It sold the most copies of anything he ever wrote, and every once in a while the publisher would reprint it with a new cover.

But I liked this one.

Just a boxer in the fog, fighting himself while the whole world watches.

"It's violent, but it's also balletic!"

I could hear Dad's voice in my head like it was playing from a recording.

He showed me the movie when I was way too young, of course. He did this with everything. I saw *Easy Rider* when I was eight and confounded my second-grade friends by talking about bad acid trips on the playground. *Last Tango in Paris* scarred me when I was a lad of only twelve. I think I was ten when I first watched *Raging Bull*.

"His whole character is revealed in the opening titles!" Dad said, pacing around the living room like he was in a lecture hall.

He was incapable of watching an entire movie sitting down.

"He's in the ring, the center of everyone's attention, but he's also anonymous. And the ropes cage him like an animal. Like the bull of the title."

At that time, Dad had been trying to tame his curls with short haircuts, but on Saturday mornings, when he waited until noon to shower, it frizzed out like he'd been electrocuted. His uniform on those days was an old T-shirt from his pickup basketball team (called the Culture Warriors), and a pair of jeans older than me. He had a bright blue coffee thermos that he used even at home, so the ink-black brew he sipped stayed warm. Dad mimicked De Niro's moves on the screen, the coffee sloshing in the thermos.

"Scorsese said he was inspired to make the film because in life, 'the hardest opponent you face is yourself.' We're all just jabbing and sticking ourselves, Ethan! Boom! Boom!"

He feigned punching himself in the jaw and staggered back onto the couch.

"Oh no. He decided to be an academic! Why did he do that?"

He collapsed backward and the old sofa strained under his weight.

"Now he has a mortgage! The humanity!"

I watched as he closed his eyes. The university was always cutting things in the humanities, and I knew Dad was worried he'd be on the chopping block someday. He was tight with money, always afraid the end was coming. But, it was okay. I usually knew which buttons to push to get him to splurge. And despite his eccentricities, I was glad I'd been born in this messy house with this particular father. You couldn't choose your parents, but I'd been given this one. He was so much older than everyone else's dad, but he also seemed happier. He railed against all the bad music on the radio and the "oligarchs" in power, but I still caught him smiling more often than not.

"I'm thinking of teaching a class in the fall that's all credit sequences. Do you think that would be too frustrating?"

"I don't know," I said. "Maybe not. They're like little movies, right?"

"Yes," he said. "Exactly, Ethan! They are little movies. You should teach the class. You can just wear my tie and glasses. Nobody would know the difference."

He was still lying on the couch, staring up at our hideous popcorn ceiling. I walked over and looked down at him. His stubble was dark, and it reached from the bottom of his neck halfway up his cheeks. I ran my palm against the grain.

"Saturdays," I said, "are the best."

He met my eyes, and made a claw with his hand. He had done this to me when I was a toddler, reaching out with his hands spread wide, saying "THE CLAW!!!!" as I ran from him screaming and laughing at the same time.

"Agreed," he said, and his hand stopped just shy of my forehead. "I don't think I've ever had a bad one."

I had already closed my eyes, though, waiting for his thick fingers to clamp down over my head. As a kid, I had actually loved this inevitable part of the game. It felt safe to have his hand there, like he was holding me steady.

"What's that bad cinnamon roll place in the mall?" he asked. "I have a craving."

I was still waiting for the claw. But a few more seconds passed and it never came. Eventually, I opened my eyes, but all I saw was the couch.

He was gone.

ETHAN'S GLOSSARY OF FILM TERMS

ENTRY #27

AERIAL SHOT

Usually filmed from a helicopter—or these days
a drone—showing a view from high in the air.
I like to think of it as the God's-eye shot.
They're often used to show a tiny character
in a huge landscape.

When I'm going through an important moment
in my life, sometimes I picture myself this
way. A quick cut, and then me, just a little
ant in the landscape.

There goes Ethan.

Look how significant he thinks this is.

17

Before the one I organized, I had only attended one protest. It was with my mom when legislators were threatening to defund Planned Parenthood, and I just went so I could write a social studies report about it. But it turned out to be much better than I would have guessed. There were signs like a cartoon uterus screaming, "Why are you so obsessed with me?" and a young mom with one that read, "If you take away my birth control, I'll just make more feminists." The women were fiery and cheery at the same time, storming down to the capital to give their local representatives hell.

I was into it.

My protest started off a bit differently. On the day of the event, I waited in front of the Green Street, dressed in all black, holding a handmade sign that said, SAVE OUR THEATER. We were all supposed to meet at noon, but it wasn't until twelve fifteen that a few people actually started to trickle in. Lucas showed up looking bored, with his phone panning around the scene. Sweet Lou came next, there for moral support before we left. Next came a few regulars. One tall, bearded collector-type who looked like a New Age Paul Bunyan. The cheese-monger from the Veggie Co-op down the road.

There were a few college hepcats who couldn't quite decide if they were waiting with us or not. They stood at the fringes, vaping and eyeing us with suspicion. I was beginning to think that this was going to be the whole crew when I heard some classical music off in the distance. As the sound got closer, I recognized it as "Ride of the Valkyries." The song was coming from a boom box, which was mounted on the basket of a Rascal scooter. And on the scooter was Griffin, looking determined, waving to Lou in self-satisfied triumph.

He rolled up to us and put on the brakes.

"Where did you get that?" I asked.

The music was still blaring.

"WHAT?" he said.

"THE SCOOTER," I said. "WHERE DID YOU GET IT?"

He put a finger to his lips and then yelled, "THE LESS YOU KNOW THE BETTER."

I stared at him.

"FINE, COSTCO!" he screamed.

He glanced over at Lou, who had a look on her face I hadn't seen before. A kind of lightness. She seemed at a rare loss for words. Griffin walked toward her.

"You actually got me one," she said.

"Now you can march with us," he said. "Like you wanted to."

Sweet Lou examined him. And for a second I thought she was going to throw her arms around him. But she pulled herself together at the last minute.

"You're not nearly as dumb as you pretend to be," she said.

"I know," said Griffin.

And then she walked toward the scooter, sizing it up. All around us passing students and the daily lunch crowd were starting to take notice. I don't think they read my sign, though. They were just watching to see what would happen next in this odd tableau before them. What happened next was that Lou pressed a yellow switch by the handlebars and the contraption jolted forward.

"Now we're talking," she said.

She got on and turned off the music. There was an actual twinkle in her eye. She held down the accelerator, and zoomed away at an impressive speed. Griffin immediately took off running behind her.

"NOT TOO FAST, LOU!" he yelled. "I HAVE TO RE-TURN THAT!"

I turned to face the small (okay, really small) crowd behind me. They did not seem to understand what they had just seen. That morning in the shower, I had practiced a rousing speech all about the state of cinema in our times, and how the Green Street was the last bastion of intellectual freedom in this college neighborhood that was becoming more and more like a giant shopping mall. But with half of my crew disappearing in front of me, I simply waved the rest of them forward and said:

"So . . . everyone, the march has started."

And when they didn't move:

"You guys should probably walk behind me now."

Then I began to speed-walk down Washington Avenue in hot pursuit of my rogue employees. Marches I saw elsewhere were a little slower, but I didn't want Lou and Griffin to get too far without me. We were supposed to be a united front.

Despite the distance, and the lack of enthusiasm from my fellow marchers, things actually started off okay. For the first block or so, we were mostly met with puzzled expressions. But there was the occasional polite question.

"Save *what* theater?"

"The Green Street."

"Where's that?"

"On Green Street."

"Oh . . . why does it need to be saved?"

"Because it's going to be demolished."

"Ah."

"Yeah."

I'm not sure we were really affecting too many hearts and minds, but we were at least making it known that we existed, so we kept walking. I tried to find solace in the story of that French theater. The movement to save it had grown gradually, and eventually there were thousands of people standing their ground, risking everything for art. Why couldn't that happen here?

"This is bad," said Lucas, beside me.

He was holding his phone camera in front of him, adjusting the zoom with his fingertips. He had been filming our march from Griffin's arrival on.

"No it's not," I said. "It's just the first battle. A revolution takes time to build. You can't reasonably expect the public to just jump on board with something. . . ."

"No," said Lucas, pointing ahead, "*this* is bad."

I squinted into the distance and stopped walking for a moment. It was rare that I found myself agreeing with Lucas, but this time he was absolutely right. Nothing about what I was seeing could be called good. Up ahead, in front of an Applebee's, there was an enormous pile of dirt and geraniums, an overturned Rascal Scooter, and a security guard screaming something into his walkie-talkie.

"How?" I said. "It's been like ten minutes . . ."

Then I ran toward the scene, leaving my small cadre of followers behind me. Sweet Lou was sitting against the brick wall of the restaurant, muttering something to the security guard. Griffin was nowhere to be found. The boom box lay in pieces around the clumps of black potting soil. There were neon pink geraniums all over the sidewalk and the street. In the time it had taken us to get there, a small crowd had formed.

"But if you've never ridden one before," the security guard was asking, "why did you get on one today? That's what I don't understand."

Lou rubbed her elbow and winced.

"You think just because I'm old, I don't want to have new experiences? Don't you ever get a wild hair, man?"

A police car pulled up on the road next to us, lights flashing.

"Oh God," I said.

"This is bad," said Lucas from behind me. "I got to go, Ethan, before these idiots try to deport me."

I watched him turn around and head back toward the theater.

A young baby-faced police officer got out of his car. He looked perplexed and disappointed by what he had been called here to do. He slowly walked over to the security guard, and looked down at Sweet Lou. Then he looked at the busted scooter.

"Would it surprise you to know," the police officer asked Lou, "that a scooter just like this was reported stolen from a Costco in Bloomington this morning?"

Lou was close-lipped. If the officer was hoping for a snitch, he had the wrong person.

"No, it would not surprise us," said someone from behind me.

I turned to see a slim figure coming from the back of the crowd, winding her way between pockets of students taking pictures. I knew who it was, but I was in such a state of heightened anxiety, it didn't totally sink in until Raina was standing next to me. She held a hand-painted sign that said, EAT THE RICH, with a picture of a fancy burrito on it.

"Sorry, I'm late," she said to me.

"That's okay," I said.

She stepped forward toward the cops.

"Who are you?" asked the guard.

He looked at her sign in complete puzzlement.

"I am a member of the Friends of the Green Street Cinema, a group of patrons for the arts. And this is a direct action to protest the destruction of a valuable community resource."

"Um, hold on, Raina. I'm not sure . . ."

Raina shot me a withering look. I went quiet and looked around at everyone. All eyes were on me.

"Uh," I said. "What I mean is yes."

"Yes what?" said the cop.

Raina was nodding next to me.

"Yes we have chosen this . . . Applebee's to show our displeasure with . . . the corporatization of this campus."

I was starting to feel a little adrenaline.

"We don't want your chicken fingers!" I said a little too loudly.

The security guard took a step backward.

"Or your delicious buffalo sauce!" I continued. "We don't want the mozzarella sticks of the oppressor! We are a vital part of this neighborhood. We will not be erased. And we will not go down without a fight!"

The cops looked at us and then back down at Sweet Lou.

"Ma'am," said the cop, "is that really why you crashed this stolen scooter into these flowers? Because of what these kids just said about chicken fingers?"

Lou looked at me then at Raina. Then back at the cops.

"Yes!" she said. "God Save the Green Street!"

The cop looked back to Raina and me again.

"And so you two stole the scooter and planned all of this?"

I was about to clarify things a bit more. It didn't seem necessary to take the blame for *everything*. But then Raina grabbed me and pulled me forward with her. I felt her hand in mine for the first time in years, and it silenced any last doubt that I should have had. I wanted to keep holding it, no matter the cost.

"That's right," Raina said. "It was an act of civil disobedience. Arrest us if you have to, but we will not be swept aside!"

Then Raina thrust out her arms in front of her and, because we were hand-in-hand, I did the same. And when I felt the cold metal of handcuffs, I wasn't as scared as I thought I would be. And instead of freaking out, or hyperventilating, or explaining that this was all a big misunderstanding, I turned toward the nearest cell phone and gave what I hoped was the self-righteous sneer of a Parisian revolutionary.

"How did you even hear about this?" I finally thought to ask Raina as we were led to the cop car.

She looked at me with an arched brow.

"I'm on the mailing list, dumbass."

18

The last time Raina and I held hands, it was in the very theater we were trying to save. After that rehearsal in her basement, when she told me about the problems with her mom, she agreed to go see a movie with me, "just as friends." Which was cool with me. I was just excited to show her something I cared about. So far, our friendship had been 100 percent on her terms. I played her games. I tried out for her play. We rehearsed at her house. I was happy she might see a glimpse of my world, even if that world was a musty movie theater with broken seats.

Before we went, I had my dad call in a few favors. When he taught his film classes, he often used the Green Street as a screening space. The screenings happened late, after the public had all gone home, but this only added to their allure among undergrads. He even taught a course called Midnight Movies that was all about cult films. *Rocky Horror.*

Evil Dead. Pulp Fiction. A Clockwork Orange. Sometimes, he let me attend, and I still remember seeing the students filing in, bleary-eyed, at various levels of sobriety.

Because my night with Raina was the closest thing I had ever had to a date, I convinced my dad to set up a screening. He reserved the Green Street on a Tuesday night for a class, but this time, the class would only be two people. Anjo would be the projectionist. He had one of his TAs work concessions. We could watch anything we wanted, but the options of the university's film archive were so vast, I started to panic as the day got closer.

If I went too obscure, I risked making the experience alienating and trying too hard to look smart and cultured. But if I went too mainstream, it would defeat the entire purpose of going to the Green Street. My instinct was a quirky romantic comedy, but I also thought that might come on too strong. If I cleared the whole theater for us then turned on a bunch of love scenes, everything might get awkward very quickly. Eventually, I went to the master himself.

"Hmm," Dad said. "That's a tough one. A date that's not really a date. A love story that's not really a love story."

"It's a delicate situation," I said.

We were in his office at school. The walls were covered in framed movie posters, including his prize possession, a signed movie still of De Niro with gloves raised in *Raging Bull.* Dad was wearing his usual uniform of a rumpled blazer and jeans. It would maybe have been a stylish look if he didn't wear his suit jackets two sizes too big to fit his long arms.

"Well there's *Bonnie and Clyde*," he said. "That's a classic."

"No crime sprees," I said.

"*Sid and Nancy?*"

"Dad, that movie is about junkies. Maybe something without a tragic ending?"

"*Titanic?*"

He smiled. I didn't.

"Okay, okay," he said. "I'm taking this very seriously starting now."

He walked over to his bookshelves, which were overflowing with DVDs and old VHS rarities that never made the transition to digital. He ambled along, running his finger over the cases, one by one. Eventually, his fingertip came to a halt and he pulled out a DVD and tossed it to me like a Frisbee.

I trapped it with two hands.

"*Harold and Maude?*" I said. "I've seen that a hundred times."

"It's charming," he said, "It's funny. And the love interest is a seventy-nine-year-old woman, so I don't think you're in any danger of life imitating art."

I looked down at the case. Bud Cort, the actor who

played Harold, had a look of complete bewilderment on his face. It was a fair reflection of the way I felt most days. I set the DVD down on his desk.

"Does the university have a film print?" I asked.

"Of course. I ordered it for the collection myself."

When the night arrived, I was nervous until I stepped into the theater. On the bus ride over I couldn't remember if I had put on deodorant after my shower, and the thought was haunting me. I had been using the same kind for so long that I no longer had the ability to really smell it. Raina caught me sniffing the air on more than one occasion.

"Do you have allergies or something?" she asked.

"Um. Yes," I said, and slumped a little lower in my bus seat.

Everything changed when I entered the theater. I felt instantly calmer, like that smell of old popcorn and orange-scented cleaning products was a natural antianxiety drug. When I thought about this place, I thought about Saturdays with my dad, sitting in a small dark room, the flutter of the projector barely audible above me, the slow parting of the curtains, then, nothing else to concentrate on but the off-beat stories my father favored.

I looked over at Raina. She had a sweatshirt on with thumbholes cut in the end of her sleeves so half of her hands were hidden.

"Don't we need tickets?" she asked.

"C'mon," I said. "Let me give you a quick tour."

I took her up to the projection booth first. Anjo was in there, opening the canister that held our print. I didn't know her that well at the time, but my father spoke highly of her taste. In the corner, incense and candles burned beneath her photo of Steve McQueen. She looked at us when we walked in with the trace of a smile on her lips.

"Today's his birthday," she said.

"Who?" I asked.

She pointed to the candles.

"Terrence."

I looked at the poster. Raina was staring at Anjo.

"Terence Steven McQueen," she said. "The greatest leading man who ever lived. So, I'm practicing some necromancy."

Raina took a step back toward the door.

"What's that?" she asked.

Anjo looked up from the print.

"Black magic," she said. "I'm summoning his spirit."

"Oh," she said.

"Yeah, so if you feel a strong kind of masculine energy this evening, it's because Terence is risen."

Anjo looked at me and winked and I felt my cheeks getting hot. She was trying to help me out with a dose of anti-hero mojo. I had only seen one of McQueen's movies at that point. It was called *The Cincinnati Kid*, and I remembered him making sarcastic remarks to this woman until in one moment he kissed her out of the blue and slapped her on the ass. The woman called him a bastard and then smiled as she watched him walk away. Somehow, sexual harassment didn't seem like a winning strategy for me. Or, you know . . . anyone.

I decided to cut the tour short and go down to our seats. We picked up some candy and popcorn on the way. Raina was still quiet, which was unusual for her. I couldn't tell if it was because she hated the Green Street or because she was regretting coming out with me. Or both. She stuck her hand in a box of Dots and tossed a couple in her mouth.

"So what is it?" she said.

"What do you mean?"

"What's the big deal? What is it that you like about this place?"

"You don't like it," I said.

"I never know what I like until it's over," she said. "So, why don't you save me some time and let me in on the secret."

"The secret," I said.

She sighed. It was a familiar response.

"Ethan," she said, "you've clearly been waiting to ask me out for months. Now you did and I said yes, and you brought me to this place. Why?"

I felt my heart beating in my throat. Was she admitting this was a date? I tried to nudge that thought out of my head. It would do me no good for the moment.

"Well," I said. "Okay. Um, so my dad has this thing about rituals."

"Satanic rituals? Like that woman upstairs?"

"No. Just rituals in general. Things we do every week. Things we can count on. He says that they make life more manageable. Because most of the time, things are unpredictable and kind of scary. Everything's always changing, no matter what we do. But if we have rituals, we can fight that a little bit."

"Okay . . ." she said.

"We used to go to church, but then Dad had a crisis. Our church got kind of conservative. He says he's an agnostic now, but secretly I think he doesn't believe in anything; he just doesn't want to admit it. Anyway, we don't go to church anymore, but we come here. At church my dad used to tell me that I didn't have to believe everything in the Bible; it was just good to sit and think about spiritual things sometimes, to get outside of all the little everyday things that fill up our minds. So, now I'm supposed to do that here. After we see a movie, we're supposed to talk for a little while about 'what it means to be human.'"

"Have you figured it out yet?" she asked.

I looked at her.

"What it means," she said.

I shook my head.

"Nah. A few clues maybe."

She looked around at the small theater. The speakers, coming unscrewed from the walls. The high ceiling full of decades-old cobwebs.

"So this place is your church now?" she asked.

"Something like that," I said.

Then, as if on cue, the giant crimson curtains started to open, and Sweet Lou, who I didn't know would be coming, walked out to her seat and sat down at the antique Wurlitzer organ. It was horseshoe-shaped and lit up like a merry-go-round. Lou raised her hands and jumped right into her signature theme, an old song from a Paramount newsreel. The projector switched on and she played along to some old concession ads that my dad had attached to our film.

"Whoa," said Raina, "who the hell is this lady?"

"The house organist," I said. "Lou does live film scores every Sunday. I guess she's been here since the sixties. She's kind of a legend."

She played a whirring song as animated Coke bottles danced across the screen. Then the lights dimmed, and Lou got up and walked back out of the theater. At that point, it was just Raina and me in the darkness. I stuffed some popcorn in my mouth and looked forward, but I felt her eyes on me. Eventually she, too, turned toward the screen. And we sat quietly as the movie started and Harold faked his own death time and again to get under the skin of his controlling mother. I could tell Raina was into that part, probably imagining the way her own mom would freak out.

We both disappeared into the story.

It wasn't until a scene where Maude is walking with Harold in a greenhouse that I fully remembered Raina was there again. It's a part I really like. Maude asks him what kind of flower he would want to be, and he points to a daisy and says he'd like to be one of those, "because they're all alike." But Maude tells him that it's not true. Each one is different. Some are smaller. Some are bigger. Some have missing petals. And then, suddenly, the film cuts to Harold and Maude in a cemetery of white tombstones and they look like daisy petals!

The shot rises into the air on a crane and zooms out until it seems like there are thousands of these grave petals in every direction. They all look identical, but now we know the people beneath them were anything but. I've seen the movie a lot of times and it always makes me want to cry and laugh at the same time. I'm not sure which I was doing when Raina grabbed my hand. But she held it tight until the scene was over. And even when she took her hand away just a few minutes later, I could still feel her warmth.

ETHAN'S GLOSSARY OF FILM TERMS
ENTRY #175

JUMP CUT

A kind of cut where the subject of the movie
seems liked they've jerked forward in time,
almost like a part of the scene is missing.
They're jarring, and they make time seem
like it has come unspooled.

Oftentimes, when they occur they're just
moving forward a little bit in time, like Luke
Wilson shaving in *The Royal Tenenbaums* in that
beautiful, haunting scene where he eventually
tries to kill himself. His hair disappears in
cut after cut until he's nearly clean shaven,
staring at the camera.

I used to think jump cuts were too much.
That they pulled you out of the film. But now
I know time can feel like that. Not just in
the moment.

Sometimes years can fly by and then there you
are with somebody, sharing the frame again
like someone has stitched you in.

19

Have you ever been to a juvenile detention center?
It took me until my last official year as a juvenile, but I made it.

They sat Raina and me in a sad institutional lobby to check us in. There were a few desks in the room, and a dour man with a bad mustache was working on our paperwork. A nearby television with the volume off was playing a commercial for a taco with a shell made of fried chicken. Raina sat across from me in a fake leather chair. Against the drab leather, she looked more childish than revolutionary. She grabbed the back of her blond hair and twisted it into a short ponytail.

"I'm trying to feel good about this," she said, "but I just feel like I failed you, Ethan."

I watched a man take a bite of taco-chicken.

"What do you mean?" I said. "That was the most badass

thing I've ever seen. Those cops didn't know what to do with you."

She looked around the juvie home.

"Obviously they did," she said.

Then she looked back at me.

"A year ago, I could have just paid off the debt."

She chewed on a fingernail

"I wasn't about to ask you for a hundred and fifty thousand dollars," I said.

"What else am I supposed to do with the money?"

I had to think about this for a minute. It never occurred to me what I would do with a bunch of money other than help the Green Street.

"I don't know," I said. "What *did* you do with it?"

She bit a nail.

"Bought my mom a house we can't really afford."

"The one in LA?"

"It has gardeners," she said, "And a pool boy. Well, he's older than me, but you get the idea. It has this crazy studio for my mom with huge skylights."

I looked back at the guy doing our paperwork to see if he was listening. Hard to tell.

"I thought it would make her happier," she said. "But I don't think it did. She likes to show it off to people, but she hardly ever makes art anymore. Most days, she just sits by the pool eating seaweed salad. I think she was happier when she was unhappy. What kind of sense does that make?"

"Maybe you should just sell it," I said.

"It's not in my name."

"Oh," I said. "Right."

I looked back at the TV and did a double take.

"No way," I said.

Raina looked, too.

"Oh my God. It's official," she said. "We're in hell."

She was on the screen, her face splashed across the Detention Center TV. The shot was in close-up from the hallway of a dark compound. Lights flickered as Raina crept toward a mysterious blue glow.

"What are the fucking odds?" I said.

"Well," she said, staring at herself, "they sold the rights to a channel that shows it like fifteen times a month, so . . ."

She sat up in her chair, and then yelled over her shoulder.

"Can we change the channel, please?!"

The mustachioed man looked up from his work for a second.

"No," he said.

On the screen, Raina walked into the blue room and up to a time machine with a pulsing light. Then, right when she was about to touch it, a tiger sprang out from behind the machine and glared down at her.

"Whoa," I said. "That had to be CGI, right?"

She nodded and then looked over at me. I kept watching

the screen, waiting to see if she'd get caught, even though I knew she wouldn't until later.

"I never asked you if you saw it," she said.

She looked genuinely curious.

"*Time Zap*? You think there's a chance I didn't see it?"

"I don't know," she said. "You were mad at me."

I sighed.

"Not only did I see it," I said, "I broke a solemn vow."

She raised an eyebrow.

"I swore I would never go to one of those big multiplexes in the suburbs unless it was to burn it down. I broke that rule only once."

"For me?"

"For you."

"Did you see it in 3-D?" she asked.

"Of course," I said. "On opening night. I drove out there all alone and waited in line with your new fans. It took like two hours just to get in. Then I found a seat in the back with a bunch of parents whose kids were in the front row. I was paranoid somebody from the Green Street might see me, but of course nobody was there. Just in case, I slumped down in my seat and put on my 3-D glasses. I held my breath all through the previews, and then when it started and you first showed up on the screen . . ."

My voice trailed off. I looked down at the gray carpet beneath me.

"What?" she said.

I could still see her entrance in my mind. She had dyed purple hair and black glasses, and she was lit from a porch light above her. She looked like a real movie star. Whatever it is they have, she had it, and because I saw the movie in 3-D, she looked like she was right in front of me. It was the closest we had been in years.

"What?!" she repeated.

"I cried," I said.

Raina started to laugh, but then she saw I wasn't joking.

"Oh my God. Why?" she said.

"Because it was amazing to see you like that," I said.

I took a breath.

"It was also kind of hard. . . ."

"Why was it hard?"

"Well part of the reason I watch movies is to escape, you know? I mean, they make me think, but sometimes I just want to get away from reality and live in a different one. I was trying to forget about you after you left, but there you were, in the one place I thought I could go to get away from you."

Finally, the man at the desk got up and came over to where we were sitting. He walked briskly with a sheaf of papers tucked against his side. His shoes made a slight squeaking sound, audible in the now silent room.

"Well," he said, "we've called your parents, and they're on their way, but until then we're going to have to hold you in a cell."

He took a step toward us when there was a sudden pounding against the glass window of the lobby. We all turned to see a man with a camera taking shape behind the window. He put his hand on the shutter and the camera took about a thousand pictures in two seconds.

"What the hell was that?" said mustache guy.

The door opened and a security guard stepped in.

"There's a whole bunch of them out there," he said. "I can't get them to leave."

"Who?" asked the bearded guy.

"Paparazzi, I think," the guy said.

I felt my phone go off in my pocket. I pulled it out and just managed to read a message from Lucas before it was promptly confiscated by my captor.

It read: **You're all over the Internet!!!!**

Then our guard happened to glance at the television in front of us. Raina was fighting a tiger on top of a time machine. Lightning was flashing outside the window. It was pretty cool.

"Hold on," he said, staring at her wide-eyed. "Is that you?"

"It used to be," she said.

He looked at me.

"We're all over the Internet," I said.

Then the paparazzi burst inside and started taking pictures.

20

Mom was not amused by my story of the protest. Nor was she particularly inspired by my act of civil disobedience. I tried to explain to her exactly the way everything had happened, but that just seemed to make her angrier. And so, as we coasted down the highway, the wind blowing her blond hair around in wild circles, I came to the conclusion that no matter how noble the cause, your mother will never be happy about picking you up from juvie.

"That Scooter was a thousand dollars," she said. "If it had been worth a dollar more, you'd be charged with a felony right now. Did you know that?"

"But I didn't steal it! It was a misunderstanding. I'm sure it will get cleared up."

"By who? Raina? Your delinquent employee? Sweet Lou?"

"Well, probably not her," I said.

Mom was silent for a moment. Then she turned on the radio.

"I'm sure you can explain all this in your college essay," she said. "At least it will stand out from the pack. The summer I ruined my life and went to jail. I can't imagine anybody rejecting that application."

"It wasn't technically jail," I said, which was met with silence.

Mom favored the local eighties station, and so for the next few minutes I was treated to the easy listening sounds of the song, "True" by Spandau Ballet, the musical equivalent of a strong laxative. It basically repeats the same phrase a thousand times to the background sound of melodic heavy breathing.

"Why didn't you tell me they were closing the theater down?" she asked.

"I don't know," I said.

"Yes you do."

She turned away from the road a moment to look me in the eye.

"Fine," I said. "I didn't tell you the theater was shutting down because I thought you'd be happy about it."

She was about to respond, but I spoke again.

"Even if you didn't come out and say it, I thought I would see a look in your eye or a half smile. And I would have hated you in that moment, but I didn't want to feel that way about you. Because I don't hate you."

"I see," she said. "Thank you for clearing that up."

I thought maybe she was going to cry, or pull the car over or something. But she didn't. She just kept driving. And Spandau Ballet kept on sucking.

"I don't want the Green Street to close down," she said eventually.

"C'mon," I said.

"Really."

"But if it closed, your wildest dreams would come true. I would have to find something else to do with my life. Like go to business school and major in laying people off. Or become a Boy Scout troop leader and teach kids how to save their virginity for nature."

"I'm not sure business school is an option now," she said. "And criminals can't be Scout leaders."

"Admit it," I said, "if the Green Street spontaneously combusted tomorrow, and I was unharmed, you would probably do a dance."

"Not true," she said.

"I don't believe you."

We exited the highway and found ourselves immediately stuck in construction traffic. I was pretty sure neither of us wanted to be in the car with the other anymore, but we were boxed in. There was nowhere else to go.

"We had our first date there," Mom said. "Did you know that?"

I was expecting something different, and it took me a moment to process this.

"What do you mean, with . . ."

"Your father."

We inched forward and then came to a stop again.

"That's not true," I said. "You went to that bar with the clown paintings and played pinball, and Dad got the extra game and gave it to you and you guys fell in love."

"No," she said. "Your dad loved to tell that story, but I don't count that as a date. I didn't know if I liked him yet. It was more of a platonic pinball tournament. And I was the one who got the extra game. Your dad was hopeless."

"My whole life has been a lie," I said.

"I knew he liked movies, so I actually suggested that he take me to one. He officially asked me out and I decided it was a date, so that was our first date. It's only a date if both parties say it is."

"Believe me, I know that," I said.

The traffic freed up a little bit, and we made it another block before we came to a halt again. The radio was playing another easy listening song, this one about a smooth operator.

"What did you see?" I asked.

"*Rosemary's Baby*," she said.

"What?"

"Uh-huh," she said.

"On your first date you saw a movie about giving birth to the spawn of Satan?"

"Yes we did," she said. "A few years ago I saw it on the list of worst date movies of all time."

"Wow," I said. "How was I ever born?"

"That's a good question," she said. "I actually thought the movie was hilarious. I think I freaked out your dad 'cause I was laughing so hard. But those old people as Satanists: it was all so silly."

She snorted a laugh.

"It was nicer back then, the theater. There was a balcony row, which is where we sat. And if you paid for the one o'clock, you could stay for the three if you wanted. So, sometimes we would go and watch the same movie two times in a row. Once for the story. The second time for the little stuff. Occasionally we went for the air-conditioning. It actually worked back then."

"So, you were a regular?" I asked.

She smiled.

"I guess so."

"Why'd you stop going?"

Her smile disappeared. We rolled by the construction site, yet another new building going up by the freeway.

There were three men digging in a hole, their yellow hard-hats skimming the surface.

"It was your thing. You and your dad's. I was happy you had it. That bond."

"But you could go now. We could go."

I watched her think this over.

"I don't need so many stories anymore, I guess," she said eventually. "I have my own. Why should I take on other people's problems, even if they're beautiful?"

She turned off the radio.

"That's sad, Mom," I said. "You're missing out."

"Maybe so, but don't tell me I don't care about the Green Street. I fell in love there. I don't want to see it torn down. If you want to save it, though, Ethan, I don't think stealing a motorized scooter and getting arrested is going to make it happen."

"You took me to my first protest," I said.

"I'm in favor of resistance. I just don't know if it's the right strategy here. I'm not sure you've got enough people on your side."

"What else am I supposed to do? Just sit down and let them take it from me?"

"I don't know," she said. "I don't have the answer for you. I wish I did. But maybe you need to stop thinking about yourself for a while."

"What do you mean?" I asked.

"The theater isn't yours. It has given you a lot, and you love it, but it doesn't belong to you. Think about what it can give to other people. Isn't that what it's there for?"

I opened my mouth to defend myself. She was basically calling me selfish. But when I thought about why I really wanted to save the place, I could only really think about myself, and everyone else who worked there. Sure there was Dad, too, but he wasn't here anymore to see what happened. It was my memories I wanted to preserve. My job. My life. Nothing else had even entered my mind.

ETHAN'S GLOSSARY OF FILM TERMS

ENTRY #175

AUTEUR

A director with so much style, they
call them the author of the film.

Think: David Lynch. Ava Duvernay.
Hayao Miyazaki.

We all want to be auteurs in life.

Most of us are just directors.

21

In *Cinema of Revolt*, my dad's first book, he talks about two main reasons why movies were so good in the sixties and seventies. The first big reason, he said, was youth. Just like the rest of culture at the time, everything was changing and it was the young people who were tapped into the new movement. "Hollywood gave the keys to the castle to a gang of young directors," he wrote, "and they didn't care a whit about the conventions of the forties and fifties. In turn, they made rule-breaking movies for people like themselves."

At the same time, and maybe because of this, young people fell in love with seeing movies again. College kids talked about them constantly. You could study them in classes. They felt revolutionary. If you were an artist at that time, it was hard to ignore the revival of this dynamic form. Many of the most original voices were finding their way into the cinema.

But there was also accessibility to moviemaking that hadn't really happened before. There was new, lightweight equipment, and directors from all over the world were making movies outside of the Hollywood system. It wasn't quite a time when anyone with an idea and a camera could do it, but it was getting close. It felt like a medium for the people, a more democratic art form in which a greater number of people could take part.

I was deep in my reading, wearing only my boxers, when I heard a tap on the window of my room. I looked up, but didn't see anything. I returned to my book, but soon after I heard another, louder tap. I walked to the window and when I opened it, a person in a black hooded sweatshirt jumped in front of the window. I screamed and threw the book five feet in the air. It came crashing down on a stack of DVDs behind me.

"Shut up!" said Raina, "Do you want them to find me?"

She pulled open the unlocked window and ducked through in one fluid movement. Once she was inside, she pulled off the hood and fell on my bed, laughing.

"Your scream was so loud!" she said between giggles. "And very high-pitched."

Then she stopped and looked me up and down.

"Nice underwear," she said.

My face went white-hot. I grabbed for the nearest pair of pants.

"I thought you were the grim reaper," I said, trying to nonchalantly put them on. I stumbled forward.

"The only thing I've killed recently is my career," she said.

She sat on the edge of the bed and watched me as I searched the floor of my room for a T-shirt. I tried not to show how nervous I was to be parading around in front of her shirtless, but I doubt I was very successful.

"You actually kind of have muscles now," she said.

"I know," I said. "I'm super jacked."

I spotted a shirt right near the bed, my vintage Ghost-busters iron-on.

"I'm serious," she said. "I mean you still look kind of like a scarecrow. But a scarecrow with muscles."

"Thanks," I said. "I'll put that on my Tinder profile."

I reached down for the T-shirt, but Raina got to it first. I stepped toward her to grab it, and she pulled it away

"Hey," she said. "I'm trying to give you a compliment."

She held up the shirt and looked at the old logo. I'd found it at a thrift store and some of the decal was peeling off.

"I'm sure my scarecrow muscles are nothing compared to your seaweed-eating LA boyfriends," I said.

She reached out and handed me the shirt.

"Actually, I didn't really date in LA," she said.

"What!" I said. "Why not? You're a new star! That's the

one time in your life when you can go way out of your league, right?"

I was laughing now, but when I looked at Raina, she had totally shut down. She was looking down at her knees. I pulled my shirt on and sat down next to her. Neither of us moved for a second. I was confused, but clearly something had gone very wrong.

"Hey, sorry," I said. "I was just teasing. I didn't mean . . ."

Her hands disappeared inside her sleeves.

"It's okay, I just . . ."

"What?"

She looked back toward the window where she'd come in.

"When the movie first came out," she said, "I tried not to read stuff about myself online, but I had never been in the news before, so it was pretty hard to ignore. Also, most of the early reviews were good. People thought I was decent in the role. The magazine profiles were nice."

"You were better than decent," I said.

She ignored this.

"But one day, I got an e-mail from one of the other girls in the movie. She'd been an actor since she was five. There was just a quick message saying 'Isn't this hilarious?' and then a link below."

I was clenching my hands.

"What was it?"

"It was a countdown to when I turned eighteen."

She paused to let the implications sink in.

"There was this clock running on the homepage and then a bunch of photos of me with close-ups of my boobs when I wore a low-cut dress to the premiere. Then there were some other tabloid photos. One from my pool at home. Someone must have looked over the fence, or taken it from another house."

"Oh."

"Yeah. It gets worse."

She looked over at me.

"I started searching. There was one site that Photoshopped my face on the body of a porn star. There were whole galleries of pictures. Somebody had taken hours, maybe days, just to make them, and they were out there for anyone to see. My parents. My friends. Anyone could find them."

I sighed.

"That's really terrible," I said, trying in vain to find better words.

She was expressionless.

"Everybody told me not to worry about it. It just meant I was actually famous. But how fucked up is that? You want to be an actor and do this thing you love and perverted pictures are just part of the deal? That's the proof? After that, every guy that came up to me at a party, I couldn't help wondering if he'd seen me on those sites."

I tried to imagine it. I had been embarrassed when Raina saw me just now. What would it be like for everyone to see my body like that or to see fake naked pictures of me on the Internet? It was a sickening feeling.

"Anyway, it's been a long time since I looked for myself in the news, but it wasn't hard to find this one today."

She pulled out a phone and handed it to me. I looked down at it. There was a tabloid article up with a picture of Raina in handcuffs. I had been cropped out, but you could still see my skinny legs in the corner of the frame. Above her, the headline read:

COLD CASE: RAINA ALLEN GETS ARRESTED IN MINNESOTA AFTER HER ICE-CREAM MELTDOWN IN LA

I started to scroll through the article.

"It's not worth reading," she said. "They don't have any information. Just the picture."

"Man," I said. "The puns . . ."

"I know," she said. "Those people must have doctorates in punning."

"What are you going to do?" I asked.

She stood up and walked around the room.

"Well," she said, "that's the question, isn't it?"

Usually, I didn't care about the cleanliness of my room, but for once I wished I had picked up a little. There were dirty socks strewn across the carpet. A couple of musty towels were coiled on the side of my bed. I rarely opened a window in here, so it couldn't have smelled terrific.

"Usually, I would just make a statement right away and wait for it all to blow over," she said. "That's what my manager would tell me to do. But there's also an opportunity here. You know that, right, Ethan?"

"How so?" I asked.

She walked back over to me.

"Well, people still care what I have to say right now. I don't know why exactly, but that's how it is. So, if we can come up with something. Something new in the next few days, I can probably make a statement."

"About the Green Street?"

She looked at me, incredulous.

"Of course," she said. "What else?"

We met eyes and I didn't want to be the first person to look away. Her eyes were a little bloodshot, but she looked better than the first time I'd seen her at her old house. Her skin looked healthier. I looked up at her.

"Why are you doing this?" I asked.

For a moment it looked like she was going to give me another sharp answer, but she must have seen something in my face.

"Because I wasn't a great friend to you," she said. "And you deserved better. You *deserve* better."

"If it's just out of pity," I said, "I'm not sure I'm interested in help."

She held out her phone again, the blurry picture of her near my face.

"Am I really in any position to pity someone right now?" she asked.

By her feet was the book I had tossed when she came in. I reached down and picked it up. Then I found my place in the text again and handed it to Raina. Her hand brushed against mine when she took it.

"I need you to read something," I said. "I think I have an idea."

22

G riffin was a no-show the next day at work.

In fact, nobody had seen him since the protest. We tried his phone number on the employee contact sheet and got a disconnected number. Lucas even made the rounds of all his favorite burrito spots, but there wasn't a trace. The closest thing we had to a clue was the nub of a joint I found out behind the Dumpsters. But this time, where there was smoke there was no fire. Just Dumpster juice.

"Maybe he went back to his home planet," Lucas said.

"Maybe he's lost in a paper bag," said Sweet Lou.

She was wearing a sling on her arm, a pack of cigarettes tucked firmly in the fabric. Thankfully it wasn't the arm she needed for her cane. The three of us were sitting in the back of the theater, all watching the screen as Anjo made some adjustments to Vicky, the house projector.

She was using an old print of the schlocky seventies

horror movie, *The Refrigerator*, and every so often the film would kick into gear and we'd watch a possessed household appliance swallow a drunk person amid screams and spatters of ketchup-red blood.

"Well," I said, "if he doesn't turn up soon, we'll talk to the police. In the meantime, this is the team."

Lucas and Lou looked at each other, then at me.

"It wasn't so sad until you used the word team," said Lou.

"I agree," said Lucas. "What the hell is this team supposed to win?"

The screen came to life suddenly and a man in a small baseball cap ran through an apartment, chased by an old-fashioned fridge. He lunged out of the way of its open jaws, red light and fog pouring from the depths of the crisper. The sound of his screams was deafening.

"The focus is still off!" said Lucas, barely disturbed by the terrifying interruption.

Sweet Lou stared at the screen.

"If anything was going to eat me in my house, I think it would be the dishwasher. Damn thing turns on in the middle of the night for no reason. I think it's possessed by the ghost of my husband."

"Listen, guys," I said. "I need to talk to you about something important."

Lucas and Lou swiveled their heads toward me, annoyed, even though I had called them in here specifically for a meeting. I heard Anjo's footsteps shuffling above us. Her head peeked through the window to the theater below.

"We all know you're famous in the tabloids now, Wendy," said Lucas. "Do you have anything else to report?"

"As a matter of fact I do."

I got up and walked toward the screen. I turned and looked around the theater, empty except for my two seated employees, and a third hiding near the rafters. I studied the frayed seat backs in mismatched colors of dark orange and gray, the long curtains on either side of the screen, and the dust drifting like snow flurries in the dim light. It still looked to me like the perfect place to spend an afternoon. It was hard to imagine that feeling ever passing.

"Look," I said. "I know the protest didn't really go as planned, but I'm not going to stand here and say it was a complete failure."

"I am!" shouted Lou. "My wrist hurts like hell."

"Okay. I know. That was a blow. But the whole thing wasn't a disaster. It brought us some attention."

"It brought Raina Allen some attention!" said Lucas.

"Just let me finish," I said.

They clammed up for a moment, looking at me impatiently.

"I get it, okay? Things didn't go right. Lou got hurt. I'm sorry about that Lou. Lucas doesn't want to get deported. I have a misdemeanor charge, and Griffin is on the lam. We suffered a lot of setbacks, but I've been thinking, and it's possible it's our own fault as much as it is the police and everyone else. We jumped the gun a little bit. I jumped the gun."

"What are you talking about?" said Lucas.

"Well, I tried to have a protest before anyone would want to join. It wasn't really a cause yet; it was just something that we were all angry about. And while our anger is totally valid, nobody really understands it. They don't know why they should care about all this."

"It's not our fault they're idiots," said Lucas.

"But what if it *is* our fault?" I said.

I was met with befuddled stares.

"I mean, what have we really done to try to make other people care about this place? We kind of just show the same things over and over, the things we want to see. And we don't really care if anyone complains. And when newbies show up, we're usually dicks to them."

"That's our brand!" said Lucas.

Lou took out her cigarettes and smacked them against the palm of her good hand.

"So what's the answer?" she said, "We start showing superhero movies? Maybe we should replace my organ with a laser light show."

"That's not what I want to do," I said.

I heard a voice from above me suddenly.

"What exactly do you want to do, Ethan?" it said.

Lucas and Lou looked up, a mild note of shock in their roving eyes. I'm not sure how long it had been since Anjo spoke to them, but they looked as if they had heard the voice of God.

"Thank you, Anjo. I'll tell you," I said. "I want to plan a festival."

"A festival?" said Lou. "Where are we going to get the money for that?"

"Well . . ." I said.

But I wasn't able to finish. The doors to the theater opened at the back and two figures walked down the carpeted aisle. One wore a familiar crisp polo and a bad beard, and the other looked like one of the Hazmat guys from *E.T.* He wore a pair of plastic coveralls, a respirator mask, and a pair of bright green gloves.

"What the hell is this?" said Lou.

Ron Marsh cleared his throat and puffed up his chest like a self-inflating animal I saw on the Discovery Channel once.

"Members of the Green Street staff," he said in a serious voice, "I am here today because some new information has come to my attention about patron safety in your theater."

"Patron safety? What does that mean?" I said. "And who is *he*?"

I pointed to the man in the space suit.

"This is my associate, Jasper. He's an exterminator who has been working with the restaurant next door, Noodles & More. They have had a rat problem for the past few months, and Jasper here has traced that problem to your establishment."

"Impossible," I said. "We don't have a rat problem. Where's the proof?"

Ron motioned to Jasper who reached behind his back and brandished a single caged rat. He held it high like a trophy and right away I recognized the captive. It was Brando! His tremendous girth gave him away. At first I was surprised he'd been nabbed, but maybe he had finally eaten too many Raisinets and he couldn't dart around like he used to.

"Jasper set up a camera and he actually saw them running into the restaurant from your building," said Ron. "Pretty much all night long. And until this problem is solved, I'm ordering that this theater be shut down for health violations."

Brando's eyes shifted back and forth with disinterest at this development.

"You're already shutting us down at the end of the month," I said.

"Well," said Ron, "consider this an early start."

"My God. What an asshole," said Lou.

Ron's face began to turn red.

"Listen to me, lady," he said. "I've had about enough of you calling . . ."

This time Ron was the one interrupted. Vicky the projector kicked to life and the screen lit up in front of us. The man in the little hat was caught in the open maw of the hell-bent refrigerator. He scrambled to get out, screaming like a maniac, but to no avail. A geyser of blood shot up from inside the fridge and coated his face. The special effects were terrible—it was probably Campbell's Tomato Soup—but that made it even more disturbing somehow. The screams echoed through the theater.

Jasper, frozen in shock, dropped the rat cage.

It slammed to the ground, rolling over, and landing upside down. The small door flew open upon final impact. Wasting no time, Brando took off in a speedy wobble making his way down the aisle, right past me and behind the screen into the guts of the theater. Then the screen went dark again, along with the houselights. And as I stood there in complete darkness, listening to Lucas laughing and Ron starting to panic, I wondered if the lights would ever be turned on again.

ETHAN'S GLOSSARY OF FILM TERMS
ENTRY #306

EXTREME LONG SHOT

Do you really want to hear about another
camera shot? Probably you don't.

You can look this one up if you really want to
know about it. There are some beautiful still
images online for you to overanalyze.

I'm more interested in the other meaning here.
The fact that most things in my life seemed
like an extreme long shot.

23

Next thing we knew, we were all in the alley, watching a man in a jumpsuit tape off the entrance to the Green Street like he was sealing off a murder scene. Jasper seemed to take great pleasure in his job, slowly unwinding the bright yellow tape and threading it through the door handles. Inside, I could barely make out the silhouette of Ron Marsh, strutting around, blabbing on his phone. Who knew what he was doing. Ordering an airstrike? Making another deal with the devil?

Somewhere, Brando was already huddled in his nest behind the walls, hunkering down for the fight ahead. Once I had wanted him dead. Now I was kinda pulling for him. If Marsh was going to shut us down early, the least he could deal with was an uncatchable rat with an endless appetite for candy. With any luck, Brando would infect him and his cronies with a new version of the bubonic plague.

"So, this is pretty much the worst," said Lucas.

We all nodded.

I looked around at my staff clustered together. It was like looking at a group of nocturnal animals who had just been flushed from their cave. I'd seen some of them the day of the protest, but on that day they'd had some fire in their bellies. Now they seemed dazed and frightened.

Anjo in particular seemed on shaky ground. I couldn't remember ever seeing her outside during the day. Not even once. She squinted into the sun, putting a hand over her cat's-eye glasses in a sad salute. Under her right arm, she held her poster of Steve McQueen, all rolled up into a tube. It was the only possession she had taken with her.

"Anjo," said Lucas in a hesitant voice, "are you okay?"

She didn't answer. She just kept watching the building, barely blinking.

"I mean where are you going to go?" Lucas continued. "Weren't you . . . ?"

"Yes," she said. "I don't think there's any secret about that at this point."

We were all quiet. A few seconds passed.

"I have some friends I can crash with," she said, but her tone sounded unsure.

Sweet Lou reached out and touched her shoulder.

"Why don't you come stay with me, honey. I've got a whole house to myself since Alvin passed."

"I've got a futon!" said Lucas. "Griffin spilled bong water on it, but we sprayed it with Febreze. Now it just kind of smells like Febrezy bong water, but it's soft."

He paused.

"Actually, it's not that soft."

Anjo closed her eyes, and let out a long breath.

"I'm okay," she said. "Or at least, I'll be okay. But, thanks, guys."

Then she abruptly switched her poster to her other arm and started to walk away.

"Wait," I said. "Anjo. You don't need to go yet."

She held up her phone as she headed down the alley.

"You've got my number, boss," she said. "Call me if you need me."

She dragged her feet slightly as she walked, just a woman in regular clothes, disappearing from sight. She looked so average now that she'd been cast from her kingdom. She was mortal after all.

"My God, they excommunicated the Oracle," said Lucas.

"Evil bastards," said Lou.

I felt my eyes starting to sting.

"We'll fix it," I said, barely thinking. "We'll get her back up there."

"How?" said Lucas.

"I don't know," I said. "Just trust me. I'll figure something out."

Lucas stepped right up to me.

"We've *been* trusting you, Wendy!" he said. "And you've done nothing so far. All you came up with was a protest with no people at it. You're our captain for God's sake, and we're dropping like flies!"

I took a step backward, but he kept his face close to mine.

"We don't have anything else. You do realize that, right? You might have a celebrity girlfriend, but we're all married to this place. My real family kind of sucks. My dad doesn't understand me. He wants me to come back to Lebanon and be a banker. Without this . . ."

His voice started to give. He opened his mouth to speak again, then he turned and walked away.

"Hey, Lucas," I said. "I'm sorry."

He didn't turn around. But he spoke one last time.

"Don't be sorry," he said. "Just fix it."

He walked in the opposite direction from Anjo, toward the parking ramp across the street, kicking at pebbles along the way, his hands stuffed in his pockets like the teen rebel from a 1950s movie.

I looked over at Lou. She lit a cigarette.

"I know you want me to say something encouraging right now," she said, holding up her fractured arm. "But I don't have much to give you."

"I understand," I said.

We both stood there another moment watching Jasper finish his job. He had ignored us the entire time our ranks were falling apart, but now that it was me and Lou, he turned around and gave us a small wave.

Lou gave him the finger.

Then, when he was standing there slack-jawed, she turned and walked off herself, cane tapping against the asphalt. Which just left me and Jasper. My crew had deserted me, and I didn't even have the benefit of staring down a worthy adversary. Just an exterminator in glorified painting clothes. And because I couldn't think of anything to say, I did what I always do.

I quoted a movie.

"You are a sad, strange little man, and you have my pity," I said.

I'm not sure if Jasper had seen *Toy Story*, but the line didn't seem to mean much to him.

24

All the shades were pulled at Raina's house when I showed up there. Across the street was a group of doughy men standing around with cameras strapped to their chests like bandoliers. They lounged against their cars, chatting amicably, eating fast food from crinkly yellow wrappers. I thought maybe they'd try to snap a shot of me as I approached Raina's door, but they didn't flinch. Somehow, I had forgotten the rules: if you weren't a celebrity, you were invisible.

I had to knock on the door eight times before it finally flew open in a plume of cigarette smoke.

"Listen, you leeches!" Trinity said.

Then the smoke cleared and Raina's mom saw me standing there, looking, I imagine, very depressed and pathetic and very unlike a member of the paparazzi.

"Oh," she said. "Ethan. It's you. Sorry about that. I

thought you were one of the vultures. Get in here quick before one flies in."

I stepped inside. Across the street, a couple of the men on the cars perked up at the sound of the open door. One of them scrambled to raise a camera with an absurdly long lens.

"Nothing's happening here!" she yelled. "Go back to your McNuggets!"

Then she slammed the door so hard it rattled the windowpanes. This left the living room dark, and it took my eyes a second to adjust to the low light.

"Why Raina ever wanted to come back here is beyond me," Trinity said. "We have fences for this in LA. Here we're totally exposed. It's like a safari."

Trinity was wearing a silk robe over a fancy pair of monogrammed pajamas, and the most elegant pair of slippers I had ever seen. She only looked like Raina when she smiled. But ever since I'd known her, she'd rarely done that. Some people, my mom liked to say, just aren't built that way.

"Where's Raina?" I asked.

"Downstairs," Trinity said, "I'm not letting her outside until things cool off."

"You're not letting her out?" I said. "Why?"

Trinity looked at me for a moment, like it wasn't my place to ask that question. And maybe it wasn't, but I couldn't help it. Her daughter was clearly in a vulnerable place, and she was holding her captive in the basement?

"It's time to get things back on track," said Trinity, "And this is not the way to do it. I've been trying to get us on a flight all day, but everything is booked solid."

"What if she doesn't want to go back yet?" I asked.

Trinity rubbed the bridge of her nose, like she had a migraine coming on.

"Imagine something for a moment with me, Ethan. Can you do that? Imagine having everything handed to you. You're literally plucked out of the crowd and given every-thing, and then you just throw it away one day because you're kind of bummed out. Do you see where I'm coming from here? In any kind of art, things move fast. I know this. If you mess up, or you're gone for too long, they move on to the next thing. I don't think she gets that. There's only one opportunity here."

The next *thing*?

I wanted to repeat this out loud. But, there was a desper-ate look in her eye, so I let it go. She pointed toward the basement stairs.

"Talk some sense into her, will you? She might listen to you."

All I could do was nod. I didn't have much fight left in me at this point.

I walked down the familiar carpeted stairs to find Raina lying on the orange couch listening to earbuds connected to her phone. Her eyes were closed, but she must have felt my footsteps because she opened her eyes when I reached the bottom. She popped an earbud out and gave me a faint smile.

"Dude," she said. "You look worse than I do, and I'm a prisoner."

I didn't waste any time with small talk. I explained what happened at the theater in a few sentences. When I was done, she nodded and stretched her legs out on the couch.

"So I guess this is what they call rock bottom," she said. "I'm trapped in a basement and you're locked out of the Green Street. Could it get any fucking worse?"

It was a harmless joke, probably meant to raise my spirits a bit. I understood that. But it landed wrong for me. I couldn't help thinking about the fact that the last place where I really felt a connection with my dad was closed right now, with police tape wrapped around it. And from there, the bad thoughts kept coming.

"I wish I could say this was rock bottom," I said. "But the truth is: I've already been there."

Raina was quiet a moment.

"Ethan I didn't mean . . ." she said.

"Three years ago," I said.

Her face went white.

"Don't get me wrong," I said. "This is pretty terrible. And I feel like garbage. But rock bottom was when my dad died unexpectedly. And then, pretty close to rock bottom was when a person I loved never even called me."

At the word love, she winced. It was like I'd pricked her finger with a needle.

"I know," I said. "I'm not supposed to say it. But it's true, I loved you, Raina. And that doesn't mean you had to love me back. I know that. You feel how you feel. But you didn't reach out when I needed you most, and that was the devastating part."

Raina sat up on the couch, and took out her other earbud. I could tell she was conflicted. This had all probably taken her by surprise, and she was already stuck in her basement. She looked like she was ready to fire something back at me. Maybe even tell me to leave. So, it surprised me when she took a breath, looked up at me, and said:

"Sit down, Ethan."

"I don't want to sit down," I said.

"Just calm yourself for a second," she said.

I didn't realize how tense I was until she mentioned it. My jaw was locked in place and I was trying not to cry. I sat down on the couch and pushed my palms against my eyelids until I saw all the colors.

"Tell me what happened," she said. "Your version."

ETHAN'S GLOSSARY OF FILM TERMS
ENTRY #14

DISSOLVE

One image slowly transitioning to another.
For a moment they overlap.

It's one of my favorite moments in all
of movies: that second (or less) when the
two images are superimposed over one another,
and you're actually in two different times and
places instantaneously.

Time has ceased to exist linearly and space
has collapsed.

25

Here is what I told Raina:

My dad got the flu.

Then he died.

It wasn't quite that simple, but it was close.

I wish there was a more dramatic story I could tell about how he hung on bravely while fighting some rare disease that has its own honorary 5k run. Or that he had died pulling someone from a burning hospital or standing up for someone who was being bullied, or even in a war we shouldn't have been involved in just so other people could nod their heads in a way that normalized things a bit. Instead, when I tell people how he died, they usually say one of two things.

The first is:

"What?"

And the second is:

"That can happen?"

I don't fault them necessarily. As much as they've been told to express compassion when someone has been dealt a loss, it's human nature to worry about your own survival. And I think what they're doing mostly is just being terrified that the next time they have a sore throat they could end up in the morgue. No one wants to think about that. There are already enough scary things in the world without having to frighten yourself with thoughts about how catching the flu at work might take you out.

But that's what happened. He came home sick one night after teaching a class and he went to sleep on the couch right away. If I had been a better detective, or maybe a trained medical professional, this would have been the first sign. Dad was an energetic dude, and even when he was sick, he usually held forth from the sofa about whatever movie he was watching, sucking down herbal tea from a thermos. Just a few months prior, he had a cold and summoned me over to watch the beginning of *Jaws* with him.

"Ethan, did you know that the robotic shark didn't work in the early days of the shoot?"

He blew his nose into the handkerchief he still carried with him everywhere.

"It sank like a stone! But that flaw changed the whole movie. They had to film without a shark at first and it's what you *don't see* that really scares the bejeezus out of you!"

It's what you don't see.

That phrase came back to me later and gave me chills. Because even though Dad was talking about a shark movie that day, he could just as easily have been talking about his own body in the weeks to come. Specifically, his lungs.

There are three main ways the flu can kill you. None of them is common, but all of them are bad. The first is a bacterial infection. This can cause pneumonia which can kill you. The second is multiple organ failure, which is what it sounds like. The third is respiratory failure. Basically, the virus inflames your lungs so much that oxygen can't pass through the tissue. Then you just stop breathing.

That's how it happened with Dad.

He'd been sleeping a lot since he came home sick, and had even canceled classes for the first time in five years. I remember I didn't want to go to school on the morning it happened because I wanted to spend the day with him, even if he wasn't feeling great. But school was sacred in our house, so that was not to be. Before I left, though, I went into my parents' bedroom and lay down next to him.

Mom was in the kitchen making him some tea and toast, and I could hear her arguing with the morning news. Dad was awake, and it seemed like he was doing better, but he kept coughing and taking deep breaths. He asked me how I was, and touched my earlobe, which is something he used to do when I was a kid. Then we were just lying there together in his room.

It was dim and cool—Mom complained that he liked their room kept at the temperature of a deep freeze—but his body was so warm I could feel it a few inches away. I knew pretty soon I was going to have to get on the bus where I would try to stay awake on the quiet ride to school, listening to a podcast about horror movies. Then I would go through another day of diagramming sentences and solving for x, trying to blend into the crowd between periods, missing Raina, and eating lunch with the same crew of sort-of friends who put up with my talk about cinematography.

But for the moment, I didn't want to move. And suddenly, I thought of a question I couldn't believe I had never asked him. I sat up and looked at him, his curly hair nestled in the folds of the pillowcase. His eyes were half open.

"Dad," I said. "What was the first movie you ever saw?"

A smile came to his lips before he answered; maybe he was playing the memory in his head, or just the thought of it was enough to make him happy.

"It wasn't a real movie," he said.

"What do you mean?"

"It didn't show in a theater."

"So, what was it?"

"Well," he said, "there was this family next door when I was growing up, and they were a little strange. The Porters. The dad was a professor at the university, which was the first time I even knew that was a job. He was an education professor actually, and he home-schooled his kids. He let them follow their passions. If they didn't want to learn fractions, they didn't have to. They could make a map of the solar system instead. Everything was like that at their house."

"That sounds kind of awesome," I said.

"I was very jealous when I got older," said Dad. "But I was young when I first knew them. Four or five, I think. Not even in school yet. I guess I had seen parts of movies before that, silly animated things, but my parents were big into reading. Movies were the enemy. Anyway, the boys always had a project going. If they weren't building a robot, they were lofting a weather balloon. But one of the kids, the oldest of the bunch became obsessed with films. He finally convinced his dad to buy him a Super 8 camera in order to direct his own movie."

"What was it?" I asked.

Dad stopped to take a long breath.

"It was a version of Peter Pan," he said. "Kind of. I saw him and his brothers in the yard filming it. Their mother had sewed them costumes, and they were the most amazing things I'd ever seen. Bright feathers and green velvet. Spray-painted silver pirate swords. Incredible hats. There were painted sets and ocean sound effects from a tape recorder. They basically turned their backyard into an MGM studio lot. There was a wooden fence separating our two yards, but every day I heard them out there, I made my mom lift me

up so I could see what was happening. I didn't really understand it, but I knew it was something wild and important."

"And they actually made a full movie?"

"It was only fifteen minutes long, but it was a movie. And
they even had a screening one summer night not long before they moved away. They sold tickets for fifty cents in
the week leading up to it and you had to have one to get
into their backyard. I begged my mom to buy me a ticket,
even though I knew the film wouldn't start until well after dark. But she agreed. I think she was curious herself.
She always talked about how 'eccentric' the boys next door
were, but there was always a smile on her face when she
said that word. Like it was something to be prized as long
as it didn't happen in our house.

"The night of the screening, Mom walked me next door.
The youngest of the Porter boys was the ticket taker, and I
remember he wore a little cap and called me 'sir.' All across
the lawn were mismatched chairs. Some from the kitchen.
Some folding chairs. Even a recliner transported from the
living room. I had wondered all week how they would get
a movie screen into their backyard, but when I got back
there, it all made sense.

"Hanging on the clothesline was a bright white bedsheet.
It was nailed into the ground so it wouldn't blow around too
much in the breeze. And set up by the house, on top of a
bunch of crates was a real projector. I couldn't believe what

a simple trick it was. But I was in awe. They did it somehow. They built a movie theater in their yard and they were going to show us something they made.

"The adults drank beer near the house. I think my mother even had one, even though I never really knew her to drink. But all the kids were fixated on the screen, waiting for the last of the purple sunset to vanish behind the row of houses across the alley. There were fireflies blinking in front of the screen. Someone handed me some Kool-Aid in a paper cup. It was so sweet and cold; it seemed to make my whole body tingle.

"At ten o'clock sharp one of the boys welcomed everyone to the premiere of the film. He talked a little about his artistic process, in what was clearly an educational assignment from his dad. Then he walked back to the projector and flipped it on. There were a couple of bleeps, and the film flickered through the reels. Then there was a group of pirates sailing on the ocean.

"I mean, of course it was just a painted background, but there was wind in their hair, and someone was sloshing water around. The footage was grainy and dirty and poorly edited. The sound went in and out. But I sat there stupefied for the entire fifteen minutes as Peter and the Lost Boys fought the pirates and won and, in this version, decided to be kids forever.

"On some level, I knew it was all incredibly fake. I knew the actors were the same boys that did chemistry experiments in their garage next door. But all of that faded away somehow in the backyard. The summer night was gone. The fireflies were gone. The chatter and laughter of the adults disappeared. And for a few minutes, I was transported from my neighborhood to the high seas. I was a Lost Boy, too.

"When I finally went to sleep that night, I saw images from the movie in my head, and I couldn't stop smiling. I couldn't wait until I was older and I could help them out with their next movie. Maybe something with spies, I was thinking. I already imagined myself as the star, decked out in a long trench coat.

"But that never happened. Their father got a job at another college and soon after that I never saw the Porters again. Still, I told myself, if they had figured it out, I could, too. I could understand how the magic worked. Out of all the movies I saw when I was a kid, that's the one that sticks with me because it was when I first realized that movies were made by actual people. They didn't just show up on the screen from out of the blue. It took a group of determined fanatics to manifest them out of nothing."

I was quiet for a moment, imagining my father as a kid, feeling so inspired. Then I faced him again.

"Did you ever want to be a director?"

He took a long breath.

"Maybe for a little while," he said. "But eventually I just wanted to convert people to the flock. I didn't need to be a god. Too much pressure."

He closed his eyes.

"It's enough just to love something," he said.

And then my mom came in with his breakfast.

"Case in point," he said, and smiled.

"Gross," I said, out of habit more than anything else.

"Love is not gross," my dad said.

"Whatever," I said.

"I'm serious," he said. "You're talking about my deepest belief here!"

"Okay," I said. "Love is not gross. Just you and Mom."

"It's time for you to go to school," my mom said.

"Fine," I said.

"To be continued," said my dad, and took a deep breath.

Those were the last words I heard from him.

To be continued.

I went to school a little late that day. I rode the bus. I solved for x. I ate a square of pizza and some soggy fries. And then in the afternoon, when I was listening to my government teacher talk about checks and balances, I was called out of class. And when I got to the phone in the office, the administrator who held it out, looked totally drained of life. But she didn't say anything. She just handed me the phone, and when I pressed it to my ear, I heard my mom's voice crystal clear, like she was standing next to me.

"Something terrible has happened," she said.

26

Raina sat next to me, staring at the walls of the basement. I was waiting for her to talk, but she wasn't talking.

"So why?" I finally asked.

She looked at me, and I think she knew what I was asking, but she didn't say anything. I was used to talking now, so I spoke again.

"Why didn't you get in touch?"

She said nothing.

"There has to be a reason," I said. "Even if it's a really shitty reason. I just want to hear it once. Were you scared? Did you just not care what happened to me anymore? Were you living a new famous life and you didn't want to be bothered?"

My voice was starting to shake so I stopped talking.

"Listen," she said finally. "Let me just start by saying

that I should have called you. That's what should have happened. And if I could find a way to do it all over again, that is what would happen. But I didn't call you and it wasn't for any of the reasons you just said."

"Okay," I said softly. "Then why?"

She slowly untangled a knot in her headphones, and then wrapped the cord around her little finger.

"I was barely hanging on," she said.

"What do you mean?" I asked.

"About halfway into the shoot for the movie, I realized I didn't want it."

"You didn't want to star in a movie?"

"I know. Just stay with me for a second. I tried to get out of it. I didn't even tell my mom. I just contacted my agent, and said I wanted out."

I opened my mouth to say something again, but kept quiet this time.

"It was too late," she said. "If I backed out, I was going to have to pay back a ton of money. Some of it my mom had already spent. So, I was on the hook. There was no way to get out."

"Why did you want out, though?" I asked. "This was before you were famous, right? Before the creepy websites and everything?"

"Yes," she said.

"So what was it?"

She looked at me out of the corner of her eye.

"My dad got in touch with me."

That one knocked me back a second. It had been a long time since I'd heard Raina talk about her dad. I didn't know much about him except what she had told me in passing. That he was only around until she was five. And he partied too much. She still remembered a night when he came home with a broken arm from doing flips off a trampoline at a pool party. There were other women, too. It was obvious. When he finally left, he disappeared completely for a few years, then he got back in touch to let them know he was sober, remarried, and a devout Baptist. Her mom had never actually divorced him.

"What did he want?" I asked.

"I'll give you one guess," she said.

"I see."

"He didn't ask right away. He just told me he'd heard about the movie and he was proud of me. And he told me that he felt bad for leaving, but it was the only way to deal with his demons. He said he wanted to visit me when I got back to the States. I could come to Memphis where he lived now, and we could eat barbecue and he could show me this youth center he was working on."

"What did you say?"

"I said that sounded good. Because, honestly it did. I was lonely. I was in the middle of nowhere in Greenland. My mom was always talking to the director, giving him advice about me. And all the people working on the movie just asked if I needed anything. I didn't have any friends."

"So what happened?"

"He eventually asked me for enough money to get started building this Christian weightlifting place. It was his dream, he said, and it was going to do a lot of good in the community. So, I signed into my mom's bank account and gave it to him."

"You gave it to him?!"

"What would you have done, Ethan, if it was your dad?"

"I know, but . . ."

"Just answer me."

I looked at her wide bloodshot eyes.

"I would have given it to him," I said.

"Well, that's what I did."

"Okay, so then what happened?"

"Then my mom freaked out. She was so pissed that I would give a cent to someone who had left us like he did, and that I would go behind her back to do it. But it was my money. And when I told her that, she got even more pissed. And then I told her that I had tried to get out of making the movie, that I wanted to go home, and all hell broke loose."

The headphone cord was cutting off circulation to her finger now and the tip was bright red. Raina looked directly at me.

"She took away the computer I had used to transfer the money to my dad. And she took away my phone. According to her it was a 'technology' cleanse, but I know why she did it. She didn't want me talking to my agent again, or a bank, or even people from home. She wanted me to finish the film, and move back to LA where she had just found us a house. Anything else was a distraction. Which brings me to your father . . ."

"You didn't know," I said.

She looked right into my eyes.

"I didn't know."

The thought had never occurred to me. I had sent so many messages, hoping each time for a response. I never even considered that she hadn't read them, hadn't been able to read them.

"When did you find out?" I asked.

"A few months later when I was done filming. Then I got my phone back, and I saw the e-mails you sent. The early ones, and then the ones you sent later asking where I was and why I wasn't writing back?"

"Why didn't you tell me?"

"I don't know. I felt totally helpless at that point. It seemed like it was all over. Our friendship, and maybe my whole life here. It started to seem so far away. Like this thing I would never get back even if I wanted to."

"So you cut off all contact?" I said. "That's so severe.

Couldn't you have at least said 'Hey, sorry about your dad. Sorry I'll never see you again.' Would that have been so hard?"

We sat on the couch now, uncomfortably close to each other.

"I should have done that," she said. "I should have done a lot of things differently. I'm sorry, Ethan. That's all I can say."

I nodded. I didn't know what to feel. The details were all scattered in my mind, forming and re-forming in different patterns. What was I supposed to do with all the anger that I had carried around? Where was that supposed to go?

"You're really quiet," she said.

"I know," I said.

I leaned my head back until it touched the wall behind me. I looked up at the ceiling. All the house's old plumbing was exposed in the rafters above, and I followed the path of water with my eyes.

"At least we're not at rock bottom anymore," Raina said.

I actually smiled this time.

Because she was right. Things were bad. But they had been much worse, and somehow I made it through those days. Maybe I spent most of them in a dark room watching movies, forgetting the world existed, but still, I made it through. I had no idea what was going to happen with the Green Street or with Raina, but I didn't feel complete despair. That was a good thing, I suppose.

"I lied the last time I was over here," I said.

"About what?" she asked.

I stood up and took a breath. I relaxed my shoulders and held my arms out.

"I still remember our dance."

She didn't smile, but I saw something flicker to life in her eyes. She hesitated a moment and then stood up too. She raised her arms.

"I never went through with the play," I said. "It . . . wasn't the same."

"I know," she said. "I heard."

She put an arm around my back, and I put a hand at her waist. We didn't have any music, so Raina just started counting.

"One, two, three. One, two, three."

She led as usual, and the steps came back, a bit clumsily at first. We went through the motions, moving in a circle around her basement, testing the boundaries of her cell. She looked me in the eye and I tried not to look away. It was really hard not to look away.

"We need to bust you out of here," I said.

She closed her eyes.

"Yes we do," she said.

ROAD MOVIE

Okay, so you probably know that this is a
movie that takes place on the road.

*Easy Rider. Thelma and Louise. Y Tu Mamá
También.*

But why are there so many of them? Is it
because we have endless wanderlust? Is it
the excitement of a vehicle in motion?
Or do we just like a character on a journey?

Probably all of that stuff.

But it might also be that feeling of being
on the way somewhere. I've always liked
being on the way even more than getting there.

When you get there, you're always going to
be disappointed, at least a little bit. But
when you're on the way, everything is still
perfect.

27

The hard part wasn't getting out of the basement.

It was getting out without being seen by the paparazzi.

We stacked a few folding chairs on top of the couch, and while the tower was a little wobbly, Raina was just able to pry the window open slowly enough that it didn't make much noise. The problem was that the basement windows were all in the front of the house, facing the street, so any method of escape would put us in the sight lines of the vultures.

Clearly, there was only one solution.

I went upstairs and left the old-fashioned way, saying an innocent good-bye to Trinity and heading back outside. The photographers ignored me as usual as I made my way down the sidewalk toward their congregation. They had only looked up when the door opened, but they listened when I elbowed my way into their group and told them I had a story for them.

"Want to know what really happened at the mall in California?" I said. "I've got all the details."

One of the guys looked up at me.

"Who are you?"

"Oh, nobody. Just her best friend since third grade."

He looked me over, clearly skeptical that I would ever be in the same room as Raina. Which was totally fair.

"Okay then. Lay it on us," he said.

"Fifty bucks," I said.

"C'mon, kid," said one of them. "Give me a break."

"I know you're going to sell it for more," I said. "Fifty bucks and I'll tell you everything."

"Goddamnit," said another guy behind me. "I might have it."

"Wait a second," said the guy I was talking to, "he told me first!"

They started digging out their wallets. And while they were fumbling, trying to come up with the cash, I started cawing like a bird.

"What the hell are you doing?" asked another guy with a close-cropped head of gray hair.

"Caw-caw!" I yelled.

Then, another guy in a denim shirt whipped around and pointed across the lawn.

"She's on the move!" he said, trying to raise his camera to his eye.

The shutters were clicking even before they got their cameras in position, but Raina was already in my car, gunning the engine. She had an old afghan from the couch wrapped around her head. The car backed up at approximately fifty miles an hour and the paparazzi scattered like ants. I opened a back door and dove onto the bench seat. I probably could have just gotten in the regular way, but it felt pretty good to dive.

Raina let out a war whoop and peeled out, heading down her street, as her mom came running out on the lawn in her pajamas. Trinity didn't scream or run after us the way I thought she might, though. She just watched, arms at her sides, the tie for her bathrobe brushing against the grass.

A half hour later Raina was finishing her ice cream on the freeway.

"Where are we going now?" I asked.

She held her DQ cup close to her mouth and scooped out the last of her Blizzard. Both of her hands were off the wheel for a second.

"You probably shouldn't eat that while you drive," I said.

She completely ignored me, taking another bite and even closing her eyes.

"Can you please not do that?" I asked.

"I know it's not technically ice cream," she said, "but this is the food of the gods. I can't believe you didn't want anything."

"Eh," I said. "It wasn't a Brazier."

Raina rolled her eyes, but I saw just a hint of a smile.

We were driving into the afternoon sun, and I could feel it scorching my right arm, which I'd propped out the window. A car passed alongside us with its stereo on blast; the bass rattling our dash.

"Box Office Video," she said.

"No way!" I said. "What's the occasion?"

Box Office Video was one of the last truly great video stores in the area. It was also one of the last video stores, period, in the area. Staffed by a disaffected skeleton crew of art school dropouts, dudes with face tattoos, and film nerds even more pretentious than Lucas, it was stocked with mostly rare and foreign films. I had been known to spend hours there, stalking the aisles looking for the perfect fix.

"I need to show you something," she said.

She gunned it around a slow-moving Oldsmobile.

"Is it *Last Tango in Paris*?" I said. "Because I saw that once with my dad and the experience traumatized me deeply."

"It's not," she said.

I watched her face to see if she was going to give me any other clues. I got nothing.

"Fair enough," I said. "Proceed."

When we got to the store, we walked past a clerk I recognized who seemed to have piercings in every visible part of his face. He was watching *Repo Man*, and as we walked through the door, we were just in time to watch a police officer look into the trunk of the car, only to get vaporized by a flash of blinding light and leave behind a smoking pair of boots. The clerk laughed, taking a sip from a two liter of Mountain Dew.

We kept walking through the store until we reached the enormous foreign section at the back. It was organized by country.

"Iran, Ireland . . . Italy," said Raina, walking past a long row of cases.

"Just tell me what movie it is," I said. "I've seen everything in this section."

"Ohhhhh," she said. "Well then, Mr. Fancy, you must be so bored right now."

She finally settled on a tape, and plucked it off the shelf before I could see what it was. There were a lot of DVDs in the store, but they also had an impressive collection of VHS tapes, and even a VCR you could rent if, like most people, you'd sold yours years ago. Raina brought her selection up to the counter and the clerk started to scan the barcode.

"Um," she said. "I don't really want to rent this; I just want to see this one part."

The pierced guy looked at her.

"Can you put it in and fast forward please? I'll tell you when to stop."

His expression had still not changed. He paused his own

movie and looked at both of us. His eyes, I realized now, were bright yellow. He had contacts in the color of a biohazard suit.

"Do you guys know how video stores work?" he asked.

"Yep. I totally do," said Raina. "But these are dire circumstances. I can't really go home right now and I have this really amazing idea for a plan I need to show my friend here. It works better with a visual aide. I'd be happy to pay you for the rental, or if you want me to sign something in the store . . ."

The clerk's expression went from sort of pissed to confused and sort of pissed. He searched Raina's face.

"These guys don't watch Hollywood movies," I said. "They probably don't know . . ."

"Oh my God!" said the pierced guy in a very different childlike voice. "Wait a second. Are you Raina Allen?"

Raina just nodded.

"Holy shit! I've seen *Time Zap* like fifteen times. Every time it's on, I can't turn it off. I love that scene with the giant ball of twine. Was that real?"

She gave him a patient smile.

"It was. We had a special effects guy build it. It weighed nine tons. The giant cat mansion was a green screen, though."

"I figured," he said.

There was a moment of awkward silence. Then he seemed to remember he was holding a tape.

"Oh wait," he said. "You wanted something. Sorry, I totally forgot."

He looked at the tape. Then he ejected *Repo Man* and shoved the new tape into the VCR. He stuck his finger on the fast-forward button, and I waited while the old F.B.I. Warning about copying movies flashed onto the screen, bathing the store in blue light.

"When I first left," said Raina to me, "you recommended this movie. You said it was the most beautiful movie about working at a theater. So I watched it one afternoon in my trailer."

I looked up at the screen and saw the opening credits of *Cinema Paradiso*, a movie my dad showed me as a child. It's about a director's childhood in Sicily, and his obsession with the local cinema. As soon as I saw it now in Box Office Video I knew which scene Raina wanted to show me. But I didn't say anything because I wanted to see it again. So, I waited while the movie went by at super speed, thinking of what my dad said about it when I first watched it.

"Sure," he said. "It's a little sappy, but it's a love letter to movies. It's gonna be nostalgic. And you can't help but get swept up in it."

Raina stopped the tape at the moment of chaos in the small Sicilian town. It is the last night the Cinema Paradiso is showing a popular movie. There's a crowd waiting in the town square, devastated that they can't see it. Our hero, a young child at the time, is up in the booth with the projectionist, watching the mob below.

Just when it looks like there's going to be a riot, the projectionist takes action. He angles the glass plate that protects the projection in such a way that the picture starts to move. Slowly it dances across the room until the picture reaches the open window. Then it's gone.

Our hero goes to the window and watches in wonder as the movie appears on the side of a building in the town square. The crowd roars with approval. And late at night in this tiny village, the town gathers to watch the film in the square, huddled against one another, the movie world combined with the real one.

"Damn," said the pierced clerk. "This scene gets me every time."

Raina looked at me as the film played on the building.

"We don't need it," I said.

She nodded. I spoke again.

"We don't need the theater."

"At least not the inside," she said.

I watched the scene play out, the tape creating wavy lines across the screen.

"The festival isn't dead, Ethan," she said. "It just needs to be reimagined."

Then Raina walked back through the store toward the door, and I followed. We left the clerk staring, his bright yellow eyes filling with tears.

28

Around ten thirty that night, there was a knock at my front door. My mom had gone to bed after making a big dinner. Raina was asleep on the floor of my room. So that left me alone to answer. My heart was already pulsing in my ears. I immediately assumed it was the paparazzi or the police. Either way, the fact that I was just out of the shower and wearing no shirt didn't seem ideal.

I checked the peephole, but it was obscured by something. So, I took a deep breath and threw open the door. And there, in the blue-white LED glow of our floodlights stood Griffin. He was scraggly with wrinkled clothes and something approximating a beard, but it looked more like an unwashed neck. His big black glasses were smudged. In his hand were two burritos wrapped in foil.

"Griffin," I said. "What in the hell, man?"

"I know, I know," he said. "You were probably really worried about me, but here I am. I'm alive."

"Um," I said. "Yes. I was worried. But also, you kinda fled the scene of a crime. Remember that?"

He scratched his fuzzy neck.

"Listen. There's no time to argue right now, Wendy," he said. "I got you a burrito. You need to come with me. The future of the Green Street depends on it!"

I looked down at my bare chest.

"This is the second time someone has tried to take me somewhere mysterious today, and I think I'm going to demand a little more information if that's okay with you."

"Well," he said, looking at the burritos, "I didn't know if you liked chicken or steak, so I put some of each in there. It sounds kind of weird, but it's pretty good. It's like if a cow ate a chicken, and then got wrapped in a tortilla."

"Griffin."

"What?"

I calmed myself with a long inhale.

"A little more information about where we're going."

"Oh," he said. "Sure. That's easy. A karaoke bar."

Since I was not of age, and not in possession of a fake ID, I hadn't spent much time in bars, let alone bars where people sing. But I'd heard about Boomtown. It was a hair and nail salon by day, karaoke bar by night. And it wasn't far from campus. So, around the tables full of drinks and mounted screens showing odd videos of giraffes running through the Serengeti, there were still old-fashioned dryer chairs and bags of pink curlers shoved into the corner. The door was open on this warm night and the sounds of an out-of-tune rendition of Celine Dion's "My Heart Will Go On" drifted out into the parking lot.

On the way over, Griffin had briefed me on his recent whereabouts. After the protest went south, he decided to take matters into his own hands. He started following Ron Marsh, trailing him everywhere, going through his garbage, trying to find out who he was and why he was so obsessed with shuttering our little theater. He hadn't turned up much at first. Mostly what you'd expect: lonely middle-aged guy, divorced with a grown daughter he rarely saw, frozen dinners from Trader Joe's, a prescription for gout medication, lots of *Law & Order* episodes. It was all pretty boring and kind of sad.

"But then!" Griffin said. "He started getting phone calls late at night to come here."

I peered into the dark interior of the bar. A mousy-looking woman in a hockey sweatshirt was belting out the finale.

"To sing?" I asked.

"Well," Griffin said. "Sometimes. He's into show tunes. But also to meet a contact."

"A *contact*?"

Griffin pulled a small notebook from his back pocket and started flipping rapidly through the pages.

"Ten fifty-five p.m. Wednesday: R.T.D. meets with a well-dressed woman, envelopes exchanged, sings 'Jesus Christ Superstar.'"

"Wait," I said. "Who's R.T.D.?"

"Oh," he said. "Ron the Dick."

He turned the page.

"Twelve-oh-three p.m., Friday: R.T.D. meets with well-dressed woman, one envelope exchanged, sings 'Phantom of the Opera.' Eleven twenty-four p.m., Monday: R.T.D. meets well-dressed woman, two envelopes, sings 'Memories' from *Cats*."

"Are you sure it's him?" I asked

"See for yourself," said Griffin, and pointed to the back corner, where a man sat by a stylish pedicure chair. The bar was lit mostly by flashing screens with lyrics crawling by, so it was hard to make out his features at first. But the longer my eyes adjusted to the light, his face revealed itself in the purple dark. His beard looked darker. He held a glass of white wine and took a dainty sip. He squinted.

"He got the call right before I came to your house," said Griffin. "So it's possible the drop-off has already happened."

Ron was flipping through a book of songs as we watched him, jotting down numbers on a napkin. Eventually, he made his final choice and took it up to the host.

"How long do you usually stay here?" I asked.

"All night if I have to," he said. "You'd be surprised how few people notice me. Sometimes the well-dressed lady keeps him waiting."

Griffin pulled out a dropper and placed something on his tongue. He must have noticed my odd look.

"Gets pretty boring, and I can't really smoke in the lot. So, these have a very small amount of THC in them. Very small. Almost none. Want a couple?"

"Uh, no," I said.

He put another drop on his tongue.

"Probably for the best. They taste horrible. Like rotten cantaloupe. And marijuana."

For the next half hour, I regretted my decision not to partake in the drops. We sat through three interminable performances, two country hits I didn't recognize, and one stirring rendition of "Who Let the Dogs Out?" by a group of sloshed frat boys. Ron clapped along, sipping his wine, looking at his watch. Finally, our lady arrived.

She was indeed sharply dressed in a blazer and a white shirt that almost glowed. She rested a hand on Ron's shoulder. She ordered a drink, and when it arrived she slid an envelope over to Ron, who protested a little, then quickly pocketed it. Griffin snapped a picture on his phone that was mostly a blur. He looked at me, lips pursed, eyebrows raised.

"So what's in it?" I asked.

"Don't know," said Griffin.

"What do you mean you don't know?"

"How am I supposed to know what's in the envelope?"

"I don't know. Steal it like you did the scooter?"

"I borrowed the scooter," he said.

"The criminal justice system believes otherwise. Actually, they believe I did it."

"Well, that's not fair," he said.

Then he administered another drop.

"Besides," he said, "we don't need the actual envelope. We can put the pieces together on our own. Phone calls in the night? Seedy karaoke bars? Envelopes? And a femme fatale? Clearly he's getting kickbacks!"

"A femme fatale? Kickbacks? This isn't a noir, Griffin."

"That's what you think! Guess where she works?"

"Where?"

"Real Estate Company. It's a total fix. A con job. When this is all over, they hop in a boiler and make for the coast!"

"How many drops have you had tonight?"

"Don't remember," he said.

We stood there peeping on them as a few performers took smoke breaks around us.

"I don't know," I said. "There could be a lot of other explanations."

"Like what?"

"They could be friends. . . ."

Just then, a song ended and the host got on the mic.

"Ronnie Magic!" he called in a cheesy voice, "Ronnie Magic to the stage please."

I looked at Griffin.

"Ronnie Magic?"

His karaoke name.

Ron closed his eyes and took a deep breath. Then he stood up with a smile on his face and walked to the front of the bar. A few people applauded and raised a drink. Ron took the mic from the host and began doing some brief vocal warm-ups. Then the song began and a tuba started to huff and puff in the background. A few other horns kicked in. Ron opened his mouth and out came a golden voice that sounded classically trained.

"Money makes the world go round. The world go round. The world go round!"

I hardly noticed the lyrics at first since his voice was so surprising. But the song, which was the aptly titled, "Money," from *Cabaret*, wasn't exactly subtle.

"Money makes the world go round. It makes the world go round."

Ron was doing a little shuffle now, side to side, snapping his fingers.

Griffin was staring at me.

"Okay," I said. "It's an interesting song choice, but it doesn't prove anything."

We both looked back to the stage where Ronnie Magic was really hitting his stride. He threw his head back and bellowed:

"Money. Money. Money. Money. Money. Money. Money. Money. Money. Money. Money. Money. Money. Money. Money. Money. Money. Money. Money."

He took a breath and repeated the chorus three more times, each time at a faster pace.

"Well," I said. "Maybe we should talk to someone about this."

STEVE MCQUEEN

Not technically a film term. Just a handsome
dude in a pair of aviator shades, who had his
heyday in the sixties. Classic antihero.

Nobody knows why Anjo is so obsessed with him.
She has never told us directly. But I have two
theories.

1) She secretly likes car chases.

2) She likes being romantically interested
in a cinematic icon who is long dead, so she
never has to take the risk of actually getting
involved with someone.

We all have our reasons for obsessing over
the movies. Some are healthier than others.
But I know a fellow escapist when I see one.

Imagine how easy it would be to fall in love
with someone you would never have to tell.
Someone who could never be imperfect. Someone
who says the same quotable lines each time,
and never once expects anything in return.

29

The next day, there were no signs of exterminators at the Green Street. No equipment or traps. No truck parked outside. And, most importantly, no sign of Jasper in his moon suit. The one measure Ronnie Magic had actually taken was to change the locks on the doors, which would have been really helpful if rats knew how to use keys. So, I was stuck outside with Raina, cupping my hands over the glass door to see inside of the darkened theater lobby.

"I can't believe he changed them," I said. "Is there any end to this man's depravity?"

I had made a phone call this morning to the president of the university to tell him about the situation, but his assistant wouldn't connect me. She told me she'd relay my message, which was, essentially: I know suspicious things about Ron Marsh.

"It's kind of sad in there," said Raina.

Which was an understatement. Inside, the space didn't catch much light from the sun. Around the concession counter were a couple objects that hadn't been put away before our forced evacuation. A new shipment of popcorn bags. A book about the anime director Hayo Miyazaki that Lucas was reading. It seemed like we'd abandoned the place Pompeii-style, running for our lives.

"It looks like one of those life-size dioramas at the Natural History Museum," I said. "You know, of dead civilizations."

Raina's breath fogged the glass and clouded my view, but I didn't step away.

By the time I had gotten home last night from my stake-out, she had moved from the floor to my bed, and was taking up the whole thing, sleeping diagonally, arms splayed like she was falling through the sky. I had dreamed of a scenario like this basically since junior high, but now that she was there, I couldn't make myself lie down next to her. It didn't seem right. I couldn't ask her if she wanted me to, and she probably just moved there because she was tired of the floor. So I turned off my desktop lamp, covered her with a blanket, and slept on the couch, curled up like a pill bug.

In the morning, I didn't hear her come into the living room, but when I opened my eyes she was just looking at me.

"What are you doing?" I asked.

For a second, she didn't move. Then she blinked and turned away.

"Sorry," she said. "Just . . . thanks for the blanket."

Then she walked into the kitchen to call her mom.

Now, at the theater, she was so close to me that I could almost taste her breath.

"On the left we have the hall of North American Mammals," she said, pointing distantly into the darkness.

"And on your right," I said, "is the death of the Midwestern art house movie theater. There was a time when people liked interesting things, but now that age is through."

Raina smiled at me, and she was about to say something else when a familiar voice came from the alley.

"It's not through yet."

Raina and I both turned to find Anjo standing there with a pair of birding binoculars hanging around her neck. She looked sleep-deprived, but her eyes were bright behind her glasses.

"Got your message, boss," she said.

Just seeing her back in the vicinity of the theater made me feel a little better. If there was any hope at all, the Oracle would have to be involved.

"You remember Raina," I said.

"Of course," she said. *"Harold and Maude."*

"Whoa," said Raina. "That was a long time ago."

"I remember every time I summon the spirit of Terrence," she said.

Then she lifted her binoculars and trained them on the wall of the run-down apartment building across the alley from the Green Street. We were all silent as she let them rove from window to window, finally stopping and adjusting the focus. She licked her lips. Then she took the lenses from her eyes, and looked at me.

"That's the one," she said, pointing to a unit on the third floor. "If it's going to work, it's got to be that one."

The shade was half drawn in the middle of the day. A small spider plant sat on the sill, spilling its long tendrils over the edge.

"How would it work?" asked Raina.

"Well," said Anjo, "I'm afraid we can't use Vicky. She's too big. But there's a portable DeVry projector in the storage closet up in the booth. It's old, but the last time I tested it, it seemed to work okay. We set up in that window and project on the wall facing the back lot. Sound is gonna be dicey, but we'll figure something out."

There was quiet for a moment.

"So," I said. "Let me get this straight. All we have to do is break into the Green Street to steal a projector, convince the person in that apartment to let us use their home as a projection booth, and then show outdoor movies without a permit on a building that's just been shut down because of a rat infestation. Did I forget anything?"

Anjo thought for a second.

"Yes," she said. "You did. We're going to need film prints. And I assume we're broke."

"A correct assumption," I said.

Raina looked from the window on the third floor to the projection booth.

"Well, I'm on board," she said.

She took a step toward the Green Street, eyeing the locked door.

"I would just like to remind everyone," I said. "That two of the three of us here have a criminal record and a court date."

The two women looked at me. Then Anjo sat down on the gravel of the alley and took her binoculars off. She brushed her bangs off the top of her glasses, and looked toward the Green Street.

"Can I tell you a story?" she said.

She must have known that it was impossible for me to say no. I had never even tried to ignore one of Anjo's lectures. I sighed and sat down across from her. She rubbed her eyes and then, with closed lids, began:

"When Steve McQueen played Captain Hilts in *The Great Escape*, his character was captured again and again trying to escape a Nazi POW camp. Every time he tried to escape the camp, he was brought back and thrown in the 'cooler.' Solitary confinement. But each time he tried to escape, he learned more about the area around the camp. And his fellow prisoners gradually used this information to design a tunnel that would actually work. His enemy, the head of the camp, Von Luger, tells everyone there will be no escape from the camp on his watch. And a friend of his is even shot trying to get over the fence.

"Finally the time comes for the great escape, the one they've all been planning for the whole movie. McQueen's character makes a valiant attempt. He steals a motorcycle and even jumps it over a wall to evade the soldiers coming after him. But in the end, he gets caught in barbed wire and returned to the camp. It seems he has been defeated. Yet, when he returns, his enemy, Von Luger, has been dismissed from his position because of the escape. And he will probably be executed by his own superiors. McQueen is thrown back in the cooler, but he lives to see another day."

"So," I said, taking a moment to soak this in, "are you saying that winning isn't necessarily what I think it is?"

Anjo didn't speak.

"Or that I need to give all of this up and buy a motorcycle?"

Raina looked at me and then at Anjo.

"No. She's saying it takes a little danger to come out on top, right? You have to take risks, act like it's a matter of life and death!"

Raina knitted her brow.

"Right?" she asked.

Anjo picked up a pebble from the alley and skipped it along the asphalt. Then she stood up and polished her glasses with her shirt.

"The Oracle has spoken," she said.

30

I t didn't take long for the paparazzi to find Raina again. By the second night at my house, there they were: parked outside, smoking and watching. Their numbers had dwindled a little bit, but there were still a few paunchy dudes waiting shamelessly for her to come out of the house. Raina seemed resigned to the problem, but my mom was not. She called the police three times. Unfortunately, there wasn't really much they could do as long as the photographers stayed off our property.

It wasn't a big deal for the moment. We weren't going anywhere. And there was more strategizing to do.

We had been dealt another small blow that afternoon. After meeting with Anjo, I had gone to the university's Film Studies department to see if I could get access to their archive of prints. I was hoping to rely on my dad's name to get me in, but they had recently hired a new chair who never knew him. He didn't seem impressed by the copy of Dad's book I brandished, or any of my impassioned pleas about the theater.

"A lot of those prints are really valuable," he said, looking past me out on to the quad. "They have to be handled with the utmost care."

I left his office and searched the halls a while, hunting for a familiar face, some old colleague of Dad's I might recognize. But it was summer and most of the offices were empty. My last stop was Dad's old office at the end of the hall. The name on the door was another one I'd never seen, and where Dad's portrait of Stanley Kubrick used to hang was now a hockey pennant. I sat down on the floor in front of his door for a moment and rested my head against the hard wood. Then a janitor asked me politely to leave.

Hours later, I sat on the floor of my room in a similar position, staring at the blank screen of my television. I had disappeared from the dinner table half an hour earlier, claiming I needed to fill my daily quota of movie time. But when I got to the couch, for the first time in recent weeks, I felt no urge to turn something on.

It was the strangest feeling in the world. Usually, I could watch a film no matter my mood. That was the brilliant thing about cinema: you could calibrate a movie to virtually any state of mind. Feeling no hope in the world:

Apocalypse Now! Feeling jaded about love: *Blue Valentine*. Feeling like watching a group of vegetarian goblins try to change people into plants so they can devour them: *Troll 2* is your movie!

But for the life of me I couldn't think of a movie that would speak to my current life circumstances. Why hadn't anyone made a movie about a seventeen-year-old guy from Minnesota who is maybe in love with his best friend, mourning his dead father, in charge of many dysfunctional humans, including a foul-mouthed octogenarian falsely accused of robbing a Costco, unsure what to do with the rest of his life, and pouring his remaining energies into saving a movie theater nobody cares about?

Where is that movie?

Something moved in the corner of my screen, and I realized someone had opened the door. I turned around and there was Raina, wearing one of my old T-shirts and a pair of baggy shorts. The T-shirt had a picture of Godzilla on it, under the words "I'm Big in Japan." My dad had gotten it for me for my twelfth birthday, and even though it was an extra-large and black, I had worn it nearly every day of that summer.

It occurred to me suddenly that if I ever wanted to get over my father's death, I was probably going to have to throw out all of my T-shirts. That or give them away. Raina certainly looked better in this one than I did.

"Hey," she said.

"Hey," I said.

She sat down on the floor, across from me, drinking a juice box.

"Where did you get that?" I asked.

"Brought a couple from home," she said. "I never leave home without juice. It's an unpredictable world."

I tried a smile, but my lips hardly budged.

"Mopey Moperson," she said.

"What?"

"That's you. Mopey Von Mope Mope."

She took a drink from her straw.

I continued to sulk. I wanted to stop, but it was like someone had activated my sulk mode. I was incapable of doing anything else.

"Maybe this is all for the best," I said. "I mean . . ."

"I loved you, too," said Raina.

The words came fast, and my brain was on a short delay.

"What was that?" I asked.

"You heard me," she said.

She looked right at me.

"You're right. I heard you," I said. "But . . . why did you say it?"

"Because it's true. And I should have told you before."

I felt an odd lump in my throat and heat radiating from my ears.

"Also," she said, "I'm not sure we mean it in the same way. But that doesn't stop it from being true."

I swallowed. Part of me wanted to halt this conversation in its tracks before it went any further, but I was too curious.

"How do you mean it?" I asked.

She sighed.

"I don't know," she said. "It's hard to explain."

"Can you try?"

She brushed her hair off her neck and shuffled it over her shoulder.

"I just don't like this rule that says love has to be one thing," she said. "Like, why is that all we get? Either you love someone romantically and you want to have sex with them and marry them and have all of their babies forever, or you get nothing?"

The first option didn't sound so bad to me, but I didn't want to say that.

"Well," I said, "there is the love you feel for . . . your family."

"But that's boring love!" she said. "It's barely a choice. You almost *have* to feel that. I'm still talking about love that's a choice. Where you pick someone."

She pulled her legs up to her chest. I watched her, unsure what to say or do.

"Okay," I said. "I see what you're saying but . . ."

"It's okay if you don't," she said. "I don't know if I see

what I'm saying. These last couple years have been really weird. I feel like I'm figuring this stuff out all over again. I just wanted to tell you that you weren't . . . alone."

My room was easily five hundred degrees now. Someone had switched it on like an oven. I got up and cracked a window. The sounds of the night came humming in, distant traffic and cicadas. I walked back to my spot on the floor in slow motion, and when I sat down, my body felt like it weighed a thousand pounds. I wasn't sure if I would ever be able to get up again.

"Past tense," I said.

She didn't speak for a moment.

"You said it in past tense, too," she said.

I got up and walked to the other side of my room, and pointed to a patch of wall beside the window.

"You see this spot here where the paint doesn't match?"

"I see it," she said.

"The first color is called Bold Potato. But when I went to buy new paint, all they had was Citrus Mist. So, now there's potatoes and citrus, which kind of seems wrong. It would make a terrible soup anyway."

Raina looked at the wall and then back at me. Her face was scrunched in a confounded stare.

"This is where I wrote your name in Magic Marker," I said.

She looked at it again.

"You wrote my name on your wall?"

Then she got up and walked over to where I was standing. She looked at the lighter part of the wall, that parallelogram of citrus.

"Yeah," I said.

She looked at me.

"Why didn't I ever see it?"

"You never came over to my house," I said. "Remember?"

She let this sink in.

"So why did you paint over it?"

"I was sure you were never coming back," I said. "And to make things a little easier. I didn't need to look at that every day."

She moved closer to me.

"But I came back."

"You did."

I could smell the shampoo in her hair now, and a trace of her mom's cigarette smoke. Looking up at that patch of wall, my room didn't really feel like mine anymore. The person who had lived here was somebody different.

"Ethan," she said, "I just don't . . ."

"It's okay," I said quickly, less to reassure her than to cut off whatever was coming next.

She was quiet.

"You don't owe me anything," I said.

"I know that," she said.

"No, I just mean all that stuff you said about not being a

good friend to me. It's okay. I understand now. You've been absolved."

I waved my hand over her head.

She smiled.

"Thanks, your holiness," she said.

Neither of us moved. I wanted very badly to cry, but I held it back this time. I'm not sure why. Raina probably wouldn't have cared. I just wanted to be convincing in my appearance that everything was fine. That I really could be her friend when she needed one. I'm pretty sure I didn't breathe until she spoke again.

"I'm pretty tired, Ethan," she said.

Suddenly, it was okay to move again. So, I walked toward the door. I wanted to just walk out without saying anything, to keep my voice from cracking. I wanted to go to the couch and breathe.

"Everything," she said, "is just so different from one day to the next."

Raina got in my bed and stared up at the ceiling.

"It's okay," I said. "You don't have to explain anything else. I understand."

She wasn't looking at me anymore.

"If it's okay," she said, "then why do I feel so bad right now?"

I stood in the doorway, not quite in, not quite out. This time when I spoke, my voice wavered a little.

"What do you want me to do, Raina?"

"Can you just sit here for a minute?"

She pointed to the bed.

"Why?" I asked.

It took her a moment to speak, and when she did, the words came slowly.

"I've been having trouble sleeping. And it helps just to have someone in the room sometimes."

I took a breath. This was something I could understand. When my father was gone, I had to sleep with the door open for months. Just hearing the other sounds in the house was reassuring. Having a feeling that not everything would be gone when I woke up.

"I can do that," I said.

ETHAN'S GLOSSARY OF FILM TERMS

MATCH CUT

A cut where the composition in two shots is almost exactly the same.

The most famous one is *2001: A Space Odyssey*. One of the apes throws a bone in the air and Kubrick match cuts to a space station, exactly the same size in the frame, showing millions of years of technological advancement in a single splice.

But match cuts don't have to be this dramatic. They can also keep a character in the frame, and switch the background, so it looks like you've blinked and they're suddenly somewhere else.

Like maybe they close their eyes in one shot, sitting up on a bed, and then open them in the next and it's morning.

31

Her hair was in my face when I woke up. I was still sitting in bed and she was leaning against me, her hair swirling over my shoulder, right into my mouth. I coughed, but she didn't move. I had never woken up next to another person and it was a strange sensation. I was hot from her proximity and my bed was a little too small. I didn't move, so I wouldn't wake her up. I just sat there for a moment, watching the room slowly brighten in the half-light of morning.

She adjusted herself in bed and put an arm around me. I looked down at it. A skinny arm with little blond hairs all smoothed in one direction. Was she actually doing it on purpose? No, I reasoned, she was not. She was obviously still asleep. She could be dreaming of another guy right now. Or a really big gerbil. I gently lifted her arm and put it at her side. Of course, I missed it when it was gone.

"Did you stay here all night?" she said, in a fog of sleep.

"I didn't mean to," I said.

Her eyes were still closed.

"It's okay," she said. "It was nice."

Then she lifted her arm and put it back around me. I felt my palms getting damp. I got up a little too fast and walked across the room.

"Whoa," she said, rolling over. "What's the deal man?"

I was really thirsty all of a sudden. I picked up a bottle of warm soda from my desk. I took a swig. It was even sweeter warm, but I was thirsty, so I kept drinking. When I was done, I looked across the room and found her watching me.

"I just can't," I said. "Do . . . that."

"Do what?" she said.

She looked genuinely confused.

"Touching," I said.

No sound from her.

"You made yourself clear last night, okay?" I said. "And I just need some time to kind of realign. . . ."

"Realign? What am I, a car?"

"To just stop thinking about you in a certain way, so I can . . ."

"So you can, *what*?"

The soda wasn't sitting well in my stomach.

"Just don't pretend!" I said, louder than I wanted to.

The room, of course, went quiet.

"Don't pretend that you're attracted to me if you're not! Because you're not. I get it. That's okay. That's how things are. Just don't pretend. Because it hurts. And it's mean. And it's not okay."

"I barely touched you," she said quietly.

"Well, don't," I said. "Just . . . don't barely touch me."

I wondered suddenly if my mom was awake. I couldn't hear anything outside the door. I stared toward the window where I could see a perimeter of sun around the pulled shade. I had no idea what time it was. I felt really sick now, like my stomach had shrunk to the size of a pea. All my muscles were tense. And the look on Raina's face was awful. Like yet another person had disappointed her.

"Look, I should probably go back to the couch," I said. "You know, so my mom doesn't think . . ."

I started toward the door, but I didn't make it far before she spoke again.

"I talked to my agent yesterday," she said.

I stopped. But it took me a second to get on the same page.

"Why?" I asked.

"My replacement isn't working."

"You mean they . . ."

"Want me to come back. To finish the second film."

I felt a little short of breath.

"I see," I said.

It was all I could say before a buzz came from my dresser. We both looked over. My phone.

"But . . ." I said.

And nothing else came out. The phone kept buzzing, stuttering closer to the edge. Raina said nothing. I wanted to walk out of the room, but I couldn't do it. I also wanted to ask more questions. Couldn't do that either. I jumped over and caught my phone right before it dropped.

"Hello," I said, after scooping it up to my ear. "Hello. Hi."

"Is this Ethan?" asked an upbeat voice.

"I think so," I said.

I was still staring at Raina.

"Well, this is the office of the president," said the voice.

"Who?" I said.

"Dan Javitz, University of Minnesota president. This is his assistant."

"Oh," I said. "Yeah. I understand. Go on."

She cleared her throat. She probably wasn't used to being interrupted.

"The president would like to meet with you," she said. "Can you be here in an hour?"

32

tried to switch gears on my ride to the university. I was pretty sure that I had just ruined everything a few minutes ago, and all I really wanted to do was sit in the dark watching horror movies all day. Invade me. Zombify me. Snatch my body. Instead I was getting an audience with the president. He didn't have much power in the wider world, but he ruled the kingdom of campus, and maybe he would be willing to hear me out about the theater and his ruthless employee.

I didn't know much about him except that he came from a business background and not an academic one. Also, he liked people to call him President Dan. The only beacon of hope I had came from the fact that he was a self-described "movie buff," and he had even visited the Green Street years ago for a March Madness showing of *Hoosiers*. In the one photo I had seen of him he was making finger quotes in the air and wearing a bolo tie.

His office waiting room was, unsurprisingly, very presidential. Lots of dark wood and gilded framed pictures of old whitey-haired deans from bygone eras. Alumni magazines were fanned out across a coffee table and the faces of success-ful recent graduates smiled up at me with airbrushed teeth. The administrative assistant took one look at me and said:

"You must be Ethan."

How she knew this, I did not know. I've been told I look like an Ethan, but probably I was just the only thing on the calendar that morning.

"Go ahead in," she added. "They're waiting for you."

"They?" I asked.

She looked at her computer where she was scrolling through photos of someone else's vacation, smiling and clicking away. Like. Like. Like.

"Okay," I said. "Thanks."

I walked down the hallway past more portraits. Finally, I approached an open door, and it felt like I was finally see-ing the Wizard of Oz. But instead of smoke and fire and holograms, the man behind the curtain was already in plain sight. President Dan sat behind a desk in a maroon suit and tie. His glasses were as round as his pink cheeks. He was somehow smiling and frowning at the same time. And when I stepped all the way inside the office, I saw why.

On one side of the room was Ron Marsh, sitting in a leather chair, one foot resting on his knee. And on the other side was Griffin, slouching in a wooden folding chair with a member of campus security standing behind him.

234

Griffin saw me come in, but he refused to make eye contact with me. The security officer looked a little bored. A walkie-talkie crackled from his enormous belt.

"Good morning, Ethan," said President Dan. "Thank you for joining us."

I was still standing about ten feet past the doorway.

"You're welcome," I said.

Everyone waited to see if I had anything else to say. I did not.

The unexpected gathering in the room had stifled any initial pleas I had hoped to make. It seemed I had walked into some kind of intervention. President Dan looked around the room then folded his hands amiably on his desk and said: "Ethan, can I tell you something I read recently?"

At first I thought this was a rhetorical question. When I saw that it wasn't, I said:

"Sure."

"Did you know nostalgia comes from the Greek 'nostos,' meaning return and 'algos' which is suffering?"

"No," I said.

I looked around the room. I wondered if he'd already shared this with everyone else. No one spoke.

"Interesting, right?"

"Uh-huh," I said.

"I think so too," said President Dan. "And I was thinking about this in regard to the situation we have here, where on the one hand we love this old theater and on the other hand we have the present, which we cannot stop. The present is always coming no matter how much we might want to put the brakes on and . . . *nostos*."

"Can I ask a quick question?" I asked.

"You just did!" said President Dan, grinning.

I pointed to the right.

"Why is Griffin here?"

Ron, silent so far, suddenly spoke up from the corner.

"I caught him in my office, going through my garbage like a raccoon," he said. "I'm having him expelled."

I looked to President Dan.

"I'm afraid breaking and entering is against the student code of conduct," he said. "So that's a likely possibility. Also, we have received some security footage that shows him riding on the elderly mobility device that crashed into the Applebee's on Washington recently."

"I'm innocent!" yelled Griffin. "If you want a real story, ask your employee what he was doing at the karaoke joint! Go ahead, ask him!"

I looked at Ron. He looked back at me. Then at President Dan.

"The kid thinks I'm involved in some kind of scheme," he said.

"You're a grifter! A con man! A fakealoo! I know one when I see one!"

Griffin wasn't even trying to make sense anymore. So, I tried to pull myself together. I looked at Ron.

"What *were* you doing there?" I asked.

The room went quiet for a moment. Then Ron sighed and rubbed his eyes. It was the first time I had ever seen his face turn red without being accompanied by a burst of anger.

"I was meeting my ex-wife," he said. "Okay? I like to sing with her. Is that such a crime? No one said divorce was going to be easy. I'm still figuring it out. We both are."

"Your ex-wife?" I said.

"What was in the envelopes?" asked Griffin.

"What envelopes?" asked President Dan.

Griffin stood up and pointed at Ron.

"Kickbacks! I've got it all on tape!"

"Griffin, stop yelling," I said.

"The papers," said Ron.

"What papers?" asked President Dan.

"Divorce papers," he said. "The divorce papers! I . . . uh . . . keep mailing them back. She wants them finalized. But I'm just not ready! We all have our own timelines for these things."

Ron looked on the verge of tears.

"This is all getting very strange," said the president.

"We used to be business partners. I thought maybe if I showed her my vision for this project . . ."

"I thought this rebuild was in the best interest of the college," said President Dan.

"How could that possibly be?" I said.

I was in the middle of the room now, shifting my gaze from person to person. I walked over to a table near the president's desk and picked up a college brochure.

"This is supposed to be a place to encounter new ideas. Look at the world from new angles, right? That's what my dad told me. To go to college so I can be exposed to things I'd never see or learn about anywhere else. Well, that doesn't seem to be happening with this."

I was gesticulating wildly with my arms now.

"My dad was the first person in his family to go to college and he came to this theater and saw a double feature of *Casablanca* and *Citizen Kane*. After that, he started coming at least three times a week. He saw all the great directors here. Bergman. Hitchcock. Spike Lee. Claire Denis. Tarkovsky. Kubrick and Wong Kar-wai. It was where he got his real education. And where he could be with his people, all sharing an experience. It's not for everybody. Nothing is. But the people who love this place need it. They need a place to be. They need a community."

When I was done speaking, Griffin was applauding. But he was the only one. Ron was still rubbing his eyes. Who knows if he had even heard me. President Dan just blinked at me for a moment from behind his round glasses. He cleared his throat.

"Thank you for that, Ethan. That was very . . . genuine."

He unfolded and folded his hands.

"There is one problem, however," he said.

"A problem."

"Yes, we sent in some inspectors after the rat situation, and in addition to that, there were a few other hiccups."

"I know," I said. "It needs some repairs . . ."

"It has extensive structural damage."

"But nothing that can't be fixed, right?"

"We thought it was just from some ruptured pipes but there are also termites. A lot of them."

"Okay."

"And black mold."

"Sure, but . . ."

"And asbestos. And the ventilation system itself is an extreme fire hazard. It's a miracle the place hasn't burned down yet."

I was no longer interrupting.

"There's also a misplaced sewage line. Some of the support beams are apparently made of Styrofoam. Don't get me started on the joists. The foundation is cracked. There's bat guano in the attic, and . . ."

"I get it," I said. "It's not doing so hot. It's an old building. Just tell me what we can do about it? Where do we start?"

President Dan blinked.

"We're going to start, right?" I asked.

"I have recommended it for demolition," said President Dan.

OBLIQUE ANGLE

A shot filmed at a tilted camera angle.

When shown on a screen, the subject of the shot looks tilted too. It's often used when the world of the film seems completely out of balance.

Do I really need to explain the significance of this one?

33

The paparazzi were gone when I got back home, and so was the object of their obsession. I expected to find Raina in my bedroom, still holing up, waiting to continue our conversation, but when I opened the door I found my mom instead. She had made my bed and she sat against the headboard, reading Dad's book. I guess she had seen it lying around and picked it up. She didn't even hear the bedroom door open and it was only when I said her name that she looked up from the pages and met my eyes.

"Good book?" I asked.

She looked down at it, as if surprised to find herself actually reading it.

"Yeah," she said, looking around the room. "It's been awhile. I guess I lost track of time."

She flipped through the pages carelessly and then landed

on dad's author photo at the back. I walked over and sat down next to her. The picture was in black-and-white and the glasses he wore were so outdated, they looked like the safety goggles we were forced to wear in shop class. His hair was frizzed nearly into an Afro, and he had only the hint of a closed mouth smile on his face.

"I couldn't get him to smile," said Mom. "I mean really smile."

I looked at her.

"You took this picture?"

She pointed to the tiny type beneath the photo. The lettering was so small I had never noticed it before, but there it was: her name.

"It took three rolls of film to get a decent shot. Your father isn't very photogenic, which sounds bad, I guess. He was handsome, though. Just not photogenic. And he told me that authors aren't supposed to smile in photos. Especially for nonfiction books. You'd never take them seriously if they were beaming like idiots. He wanted to look serious. Even though he wasn't."

"He could pretend," I said.

"Yeah, he could," she said.

She set the book down and looked out the window to the empty street. All the paparazzi cars had abandoned their posts. There were only a few fast-food wrappers to prove they'd ever been there at all.

"He almost gave it all up," she said.

"Gave what up?" I said.

"Writing. Teaching. Film stuff. All of it."

"Why?" I asked.

"Well, when you were born, he didn't have a teaching job yet, and he wasn't certain he would ever get one. He hadn't published his book, and there were very few openings. But there was a job opening for a technical writer. It was writing manuals for farming equipment. But it was a good salary and benefits. It was a good job on paper, one a lot of people would have been happy to have, especially in a tough economy.

"He went to the interview and they liked him. He was charming. He was a good writer. They offered him the job and he asked if he could have the weekend to think about it. I was home with you at the time, and I was still trying to find work. His graduate school stipend wasn't enough to live on really, not with a baby. Things were getting tight. We didn't talk much about the job at first. He holed up inside his office, working on the concluding chapter of his book. He came out to spend time with you. You had colic at the time. You wanted to be held constantly or you cried louder than any baby I had ever heard. So he took his turn, walking you around. Singing to you. And eventually, he started talking to you about his dilemma. He talked to you like you were already an adult. It didn't matter that you didn't reply.

"I can still hear him having it out with you, walking circles around the tiny living room in our student housing complex. 'Ethan,' he said, 'here's the deal, little man. I want to give you everything I can. Every single thing. I don't want your life to be bad or sad, you know? The thought of not having diaper money for you makes me want to cry. I have cried. Just like you. But, if I give up who I am for you, I don't know what kind of dad I'm going to be. I might be one of those guys you see at the Little League game, staring off in the distance, trying to figure out who he's become. But I don't want to be that dad. I want to be the dad that's excited to get up in the morning, and wants to share everything I love with you. I don't want to make short term decisions that take me away from that.'

"You were quiet the whole time," Mom said. "Just the sound of his voice was calming to you, but you also had this wide-eyed look on your face, like you were taking in the whole predicament and you wanted to help. And he started walking faster and bouncing you a little bit, and he said, 'Just tell me what I should do? You want the easy money? You want the fancy baby food and the bouncy chair that costs as much as our couch? Should I write about the tractors? Get that easy tractor money? So people can clearly understand how to bale some hay? Is that what I should do?'

"You looked at him," Mom said. "And you squinted your

eyes. He had stopped walking and you seemed calm for a moment. The house was the quietest it had been in weeks. And then you scrunched up your face, and your cheeks turned red and you started to scream as loud as I had ever heard. You wailed. We could hear the next-door neighbors complaining to each other. And your dad looked at me and smiled.

"And the next week, he went back to his book and took a morning job cleaning parking garages so his evenings would be free to write. And eventually, his book came out and his old mentor called him back to teach where he'd gone to school. But if you hadn't cried, he might have spent his life writing about combine attachments."

"So I saved his career, basically."

"Basically," she said. "Though, he kind of stacked the deck since all you ever did was cry. But still, it was an especially loud one that time. A persuasive argument."

I rested my head against my mom's shoulder. It was something I hadn't done in a long time—I couldn't remember the last time actually. I forgot how safe it made me feel. But with this sense of comfort came the tears I had been holding in since yesterday. They were for a lot of things, but first among them was that the madman in shop glasses was no longer in my life.

"I feel like if he was still here, he would know exactly what to do," I said. "He would know who to talk to and what to say to keep the Green Street going. Everything I've tried has failed. Like spectacularly failed. I've ruined his legacy."

My mom didn't say anything for a minute. She reached over and grabbed a Kleenex and handed it to me. Then she grabbed another one for herself.

"You haven't ruined anything. Your dad and that theater aren't the same thing. One is a person. One is a place. Places change. They don't stay the same no matter what you do. He knew that better than anyone."

"I don't want it to change. I don't want anything to change anymore."

I didn't finish. She slung an arm around me.

"That's not possible," she said.

She looked out the window where Raina's stalkers used to be.

"Everything isn't over yet," she said. "The building is still standing."

"For now," I said.

"Still," she said, "there are different kinds of victories."

"What do you mean?" I asked.

"Well," she said, turning the book around so we looked down at the cover. "Take your dad's favorite movie."

She pointed down at De Niro on the cover, his gloves at his sides.

"In boxing it's not always a knockout, right? Knockouts are actually kind of rare. Most of the time, it's a Technical

Knockout, or a Split Decision. There's even some respect in completing all the fight's rounds. It's called "going the distance."

"How do you know so much about boxing?"

"Your dad made me watch that movie a hundred times when he was writing the book. I picked up a few things."

"Going the distance," I said.

"If they never knock you out," she said, "they don't really win."

I looked around the room. The Godzilla T-shirt that Raina wore was at the foot of the bed.

"I didn't hear her leave," my mom said.

"Who?" I said.

My mom gave me a look.

"I talked to her mom, though. Sounds like she's getting another shot at the film."

"Yeah," I said. "Who else is going to stop the time-traveling cats?"

"When I woke up, she was out in the street," Mom said. "I was at the window, and I saw her go right up to the paparazzi. She didn't even try to hide. She just approached them and let them take some pictures. Then she talked to them for almost ten minutes before a cab showed up and drove her away. Now, what do you think that was all about?"

34

I was online in minutes, looking up Raina's Twitter feed. She hadn't posted much since her meltdown in Culver City, but of course, other people had been tweeting at her, mentioning her name, here and there. So, she stayed alive on social media, whether she was there or not. There were the concerned fans—*Raina, we love you, feel better!*—and the usual army of trolls—*Another child actor gone crazy. Who would have guessed?*—but at the top was a tweet that was only an hour old: *A once in a lifetime opportunity at the Green Street Cinema in Minneapolis tomorrow. Stay tuned for instructions!*

I stared at the words for a moment. We hadn't planned anything yet. And as far as I knew, Raina was already on a plane back to Hollywood. But my heart was pounding. What was she talking about? I called Raina's phone, but it went right to voice mail. I paced my room, only stopping to pick up the folded T-shirt, which smelled like her shampoo. I was about to get in bed and pull the covers over my head when I got a text from Anjo telling me to meet her at the theater.

"**Come through the Alley,**" she said. "**The password is Terrence.**"

"**Password? What's going on?**" I wrote back, but again, got no answer.

Fifteen minutes later, I parked down the street from the cinema. I walked past the taped-off front doors and the ghost lobby inside. I continued on toward the alley, where the Dumpsters sat in their usual spots near the building. It was quiet, and no one was around. I guess if they were going to tear the place down, there was no real reason to bring the exterminators in. The rats would be wiped out along with my memories. I stood around for a moment or two, looking for Anjo, but I saw no trace of her. So I stood in the middle of the alleyway, closed my eyes, and said:

"Terrence?"

I don't know what I was expecting. A magical spell? A genie? But I heard a single window fly open above me. I opened my eyes and saw a shadow move past it. Then a rope ladder flopped over the side of the window. It was the kind you might use to get into a kid's tree house in an idyllic small town. It hung down, perfectly straight, coming to rest just inches from the ground.

I looked around to see if anyone else had seen what I'd seen. But I was alone. So, without anything else I could think to do, I grabbed onto the first rung and pulled myself up. It was a little wobbly, and I wondered as I took more than one step, if this was the way it would all end for me, falling two stories and breaking my back near the site of my biggest disappointment.

When I got to the final rung, I looked inside and found an outstretched hand waiting for me. It was Lucas. He grabbed me by the wrist and helped to pull me into the projection booth. We both collapsed onto the dusty floor, and when I looked up, there were Griffin and Anjo, peering down on me.

"Wendy!" said Griffin from above me. "So glad you could make it."

I stood up and brushed the dust bunnies out of my hair.

"How did you guys get in here?" I asked. "The place is still locked, right?"

Anjo seemed disappointed by the question.

"You think a locked door can keep me out?" she asked. "I lived here for ten years. I was climbing those Dumpsters when you had your baby teeth."

"I came in the back door," added Griffin. "I have a thing about high places."

"That's ironic," said Lucas.

Griffin tossed a wad of paper at him.

"So," I said. "It's really great to see you guys. But what exactly are we doing here? This place is set for demolition."

"Not tonight, it's not," said Griffin. "And not tomorrow."

Anjo stepped forward. She was carrying a gray film canister, coated in dust.

"What's that?" I asked.

She had a serious look on her face.

"Maybe it's better if I show you," she said.

I dropped myself into one of the broken theater seats and let out a long breath. Perfect discomfort. I could feel a rogue spring against the small of my back, and the fabric was nearly gone from the armrests. Hours ago, I wasn't sure I would ever be in one of these seats again, and now here I was. I sat three rows back, looking at the old screen. Griffin and Lucas were on either side of me. And when the curtains parted, a door in the back of the theater cracked open and Sweet Lou appeared, shrouded in the lobby's sunlight, like she was dropping in from the afterlife.

"Will somebody hold this goddamn thing open for me?" she asked. "I have one functioning arm."

Lucas jumped up to get the door. Then Lou walked slowly down the aisle like a bride going to meet her soul mate, except this bride had a cigarette burning between her lips and her soul mate was an organ. When she got to the bench, she rubbed her smoke out against her boot heel, and cracked her knuckles one at a time. She fired up the Wurlitzer, and a smile came to her face.

She gently removed her arm from its sling and let her hands rest on the keys. A great booming whir from the lower keys echoed through the space. She turned down the volume and settled into a simple melody. Above me, I heard Anjo's voice calling down.

"When we first got shut down," she said, "I sent word to Randy."

I put a hand to my brow and stared up into the lights of the booth, but I couldn't see her.

"How?" I said. "How did you find him?"

"The Oracle knows all," she said.

Then when nobody questioned her:

"Jesus, guys. He left me an emergency number."

"Huh," said Griffin.

"I figured that was the time to use it," she said. "I told him what happened and he wasn't surprised. He knew we were done for, I guess. He just didn't want to tell us any sooner than he had to. But when I told him we wanted to have one last showing, he said he had something for you, Ethan."

"For me?"

"He specifically mentioned you. And he sent me this."

"What is it?" I said.

"I'm just . . ." she said. "It's better if you see it."

And with that, she flicked the switch and Vicky, the house projector, popped to life like she'd never taken a break. The leader whipped through, and the film stock was so scratchy, I could barely see anything. But there was nothing to see yet. Just light dancing on the screen. Then gradually, something came into focus.

It was a man walking down a street. At first we just see his shoes, some old tarnished wingtips. Nothing special. The shot is from above, shoes stomping across wet pavement after a rain. The puddles reflect the clouds and it looks like there's a sky in each square of sidewalk.

And then just when things are starting to get into a rhythm, the person steps in a mud puddle. It soaks his shoe all the way through and he tries to shake it off, but it's so waterlogged it doesn't make a difference. But he keeps walking.

Then he tries to cross the street, and just when he puts a foot down on the road, a bicycle runs over his shoe. He takes a step back, and you see his hands go down to hug his foot. He's hopping on one foot. Then he gives it another try, and the shoes cross the street to the other side. The camera lifts up a little so we can see the street.

"Hey," said Lucas, "isn't that Washington Avenue?"

And it was. Only a different version, like Washington

Avenue from another dimension. Instead of all the chain stores, there were just some dusty storefronts that looked like local businesses and old apartments. And there was no sign of the light rail, which was so prominent in the current version. But even from a tight bird's-eye view, the street was recognizable.

"He's walking toward Green Street," said Lucas now.

It was true. The wingtips were headed our way. And just when the shoes got to the corner of our street, they stepped in gum. The shoes stumbled a bit, then the hand came in and plucked the gum off. The shoes scuffed the sidewalk a bit and then kept going. They picked up their pace now, clipping across the sidewalk until they finally reached the glass doors.

The glass doors of our theater.

The facade looked a lot better. What we could see of it, anyway. The glass was shiny, and when the shoes stepped inside, the carpet didn't look so worn. A ticket dropped into the frame and the hand reached down to pick it up. Then the shoes picked up the pace and ran through the lobby and into the very theater we were sitting in. The curtains billowed at the side of the screen. The empty seats looked like new red sweaters. And then the camera finally tilted up and met the face of a woman.

My mother.

She was much younger, but I recognized her immediately. The little gap between her teeth. I had never thought so before, but she did look like Monica Vitti. She swept a hair from her face and tucked it behind her ear. "You're late," she mouthed, and then in a classic reverse shot, I saw a man with terrible glasses. A man with a head of manic curls and dark eyebrows. He smiled for just a second. I only had a moment to see his face with the light of a film shining on it. And it looked like my face. He must have been younger than in his author photo. College-aged.

Not much older than me.

The camera tilted back down to his feet, where for just a second, they entangled with my mother's, and the light of the film flickered against them. But I was still seeing my dad's face, my face in front of me. He said he never wanted to be a director.

But he never threw away his film. He had given it to Randy for his archive. And now Randy had dug it up and sent it here. It couldn't have been much longer than a minute or two, but there it was. My dad's filmmaking debut and swan song all in one reel, up on the screen of the Green Street.

"Anjo!" said Lucas. "Something is wrong with Ethan. He's moving his mouth without saying anything."

I leaned back in my seat and closed my eyes.

"That's *it*?" said Griffin. "That was the whole thing?"

Sweet Lou was no longer playing the organ. She knew who had been on the screen. And above me Anjo was silent. She had already watched it.

"I thought it was kind of cool," said Lucas. "I mean the fashion was ridiculous, but . . ."

"Has anybody else seen this?" I yelled up to Anjo.

"Like who?" said Griffin.

"Anjo!" I said. "Has Raina seen this?"

Anjo leaned her head out of the booth.

"No," she said. "But I told her about it. I was trying to get ahold of you, so I may have said something."

I nodded.

"I think I know what she's up to," I said.

Sweet Lou looked at me.

"What are you talking about? Are we still having a festival?" she asked.

"I think we're doing something better," I said.

I got up out of my seat, pulling my phone out as I approached the exit.

ETHAN'S GLOSSARY OF FILM TERMS

ENTRY #83

GUERRILLA FILMMAKING

Making a movie on the smallest budget
imaginable.

A tiny crew. Real locations. No permits. No
name actors. Maybe an iPhone and a microphone.

Purists will say these aren't real movies.
That there's a certain standard of quality to
adhere to.

But maybe it's time to break down the last
of those walls.

35

"You don't need the theater and you don't need prints," she said.

I just listened. It had taken three consecutive calls, but she had finally picked up.

"Where are you?" I asked. "I thought you were leaving."

"Still here," she said. "Midnight tomorrow I turn into a pumpkin. Did you hear what I said?"

"I did. You want people to make their own films, right?"

"Yes," she said. "How did you know?"

"Just a guess."

"I've seen these festivals in LA," she said. "We give the public twenty-four hours to make a one-minute film. Then we screen them tomorrow."

She sounded excited. I think I was, too, but it was weird to be talking to her again. It seemed like this morning had never happened.

"Do you think people are actually going to do it?" I asked. "Are they going to enter this festival with such short notice?"

"They will if there's a celebrity judge," she said.

I couldn't help but smile a little.

"Are you sure you can make it?" I asked. "I mean, with your flight."

"It's gonna be tight, but I think so. Maybe this will give you some attention. Change some minds. I'm not going to miss that."

I wanted to tell her about what I'd been told at the president's office, but I didn't have the heart. Not when she had already put in so much effort.

"Yeah," I said. "I hear you. It's exciting."

She was waiting for me to say more. But I couldn't.

"So, you're flying out at midnight?" I asked.

"Mom booked us on a red-eye." She sighed. "It was the soonest we could get seats in first class."

"How is your mom?" I asked.

"Not happy with me," she said. "But happy to be leaving here, I guess."

"How about you?" I asked.

"What about me?"

"Are you happy to be leaving?"

I waited a few seconds, but she didn't answer. I heard her typing something at her computer.

"I'm about to send out instructions for the festival."

When I didn't answer, she said:

"How was your dad's film?"

"I don't know," I said. "It was so weird to see it. I think it was good. It was good he did it. I'm happy about that. But it was too much to process right now."

Another pause.

"Listen," I said, "about this morning . . ."

"Ethan," she said, "I know there's a lot to get done for the festival. But I might not be back in town for a while."

I could hear her take a couple of breaths, the light sound coming through the phone.

"Okay," I said. "What do you want to do?"

"I thought maybe we could watch a movie," she said. "Your pick."

I went to Box Office Video alone, and it was as dark as ever. Despite the sun outside, it took a minute for my eyes to adjust to the light. It was similar to the feeling of going to a matinee on a hot summer day. When the lights went down, you could magically create that nighttime feeling in the middle of the day. An erasure of all that daytime order. It opened up your mind to new possibilities, new realities. Box Office Video was a testament to that feeling. They gave you permission to extinguish the day.

Either that, or they were too cheap to pay their light bill.

The same clerk was behind the counter as last time. He sort of nodded at me when I entered, his eyes only unfastening from the screen for less than a second. I wandered through the store, past the familiar racks of cult classics and experimental shorts and down into the basement where I knew they had the entire Criterion Collection on a wall at the back. Lucas claims to have seen four hundred of the total nine hundred volumes. But I think he's rounding up.

I searched for the film I wanted, number 549 in the series. *The Last Picture Show* by Peter Bogdanovich.

What can I say; it just seemed right.

And there it was, next to a couple of films I'd never heard of (though I would never admit that to Lucas). I grabbed the case and forced myself not to browse. I made my way back to the front of the store and placed it on the counter. The clerk with the piercings looked at me and then picked up the case.

"Do you actually want to rent something this time?"

I hadn't been sure that he recognized me.

"Yeah," I said. "Just a standard rental please. Unless you're inviting me . . ."

"I'm not," he said.

I handed him my card with the barcode nearly eroded. He scanned it and went off to get the actual disc. Up until now, I had paid no attention to what he was watching, but when he left, I looked up at the screen and, of course, there was Raina. Again. Surrounded by evil cats. On the screen, she was standing at the door to a glowing portal. She had the chosen kitten in her arms, and a look of steely determination on her face. She was standing between two worlds, deciding which one to stay in. You could see the agony on her face.

"Don't go," I said to myself. "The cats need you."

"Go!" said the clerk, who had just reappeared. "Save yourself for the sequel!"

There was almost a smile on his face as he handed me my disc.

"I can't believe you're friends with her," he said. "I mean, I knew she grew up here, but it's hard to see her as a real person, you know? Is it weird being friends with a celebrity?"

"A little," I said.

The clerk kept talking.

"The next time you see her," he said. "Tell her she can rent here for free. I talked to the manager and he's cool with it."

"You can tell her yourself," I said.

His eyes turned to slits.

"There's something happening at the Green Street tomorrow. You can find the details online. It might be something you're interested in."

Raina screamed out from the screen above us, and we both cocked our heads to watch as she jumped headlong into the portal, disappearing into another dimension, not knowing if she would ever see her home planet again.

"Thanks for the movie," I said.

My mom was still at work when Raina reappeared in my kitchen. We had the place to ourselves. We didn't say much to each other as I made some microwave popcorn and Raina melted the butter, stirring it slowly with a spoon. We decided to watch the movie in the living room on the good TV, and when we got to the couch I finally spoke up.

"My dad had these rules when we went to the movies. Do you want to hear them?"

"Okay," she said.

"There are just two. Number one, when it's over, you have to tell me the image from the film that you just can't shake. And then, number two, you have to tell me what you think of the last line."

She nodded and took a bite of popcorn, and I knew I was supposed to start the movie, but I snuck a look at her. She looked different to me now that she was going back. She was wearing slightly nicer clothes, for one, a dress today with green and blue stripes. And her hair was in a new style. A few long strands covered part of her right eye. I felt like she had been in disguise as a normal person the whole time she was back, but now she was preparing to reenter a world where she had to stand out again.

I didn't know where to sit, so I chose the cushion on the far right. She sat on the left side and put the popcorn in the middle between us.

"Listen, Ethan," she said. "I know we need to talk. But right now, can we just watch this movie together. Is that okay?"

I relaxed my shoulders and picked up the remote.

"Yeah," I said. "It's okay."

Then I pressed play and *The Last Picture Show* started. I don't know if you've seen it. I wouldn't blame you if you haven't. It's kind of slow and moody. It was made in 1971 and it's the kind of movie the Green Street shows. But it kills me every time.

It's about these high school kids in North Texas in the 1950s, and there's really not much of a plot in a traditional sense. It's a poor town, and there's nothing to do except go to the movies or shoot pool before you grow up and work as a roughneck in the oil fields. But most of the people in the movie just get their hearts broken over and over again. There's nothing else to do. Except go to the movies.

The film begins and ends with the same shot of the movie theater. Only they call it the "picture show." In the beginning, someone's climbing up a ladder to put letters on the marquee by hand. And by the end of the movie, the man who owns the theater has died and it's shuttered in the middle of a sandstorm. The movie is in black-and-white, and the main character, a kid named Sonny, is just trying to make sense of it all.

But there's a part I love where it's the last night the movie theater is going to be open and two old friends decide to go. Sonny is one of them, and his friend Duane is another. Duane has joined the army and he's about to get sent to Korea. It's his last night in town before he catches the bus in the morning. They got in a fight the last time he was in town because they were in love with the same girl, but now she didn't choose either of them and she went off to college.

So they do what they always do: go to the movies. Only now it's the last one ever. And it's Duane's last night, and they might never see each other again. But they go and they watch a Western in a nearly deserted theater. And when we see them, they're eating popcorn and staring at the screen, completely lost in the film. The theater's a little smoky and you can see the light pouring out of the projection booth above them like something divine. And then the houselights come on and they stumble out into the lobby, and if you look closely at the frame, there are signs that say "Coming Soon," and "Starts Saturday," but there are no movies listed.

When it ended, Raina and I just sat on the couch watching the black screen.

"I didn't think today could get any more depressing," she said.

"I know," I said. "It's not super uplifting."

I looked at her across the couch. She smiled.

"Okay," she said. "I know the answers."

It took me a second to catch up.

"To your dad's questions."

"Let's hear them," I said.

"The image I can't shake is of that kid who can't talk."

"Billy," I said.

"Billy," she said. "It's the image of Billy sweeping off the street in the middle of a sandstorm. It was so haunting. And I think I know what that feels like. Like it's all swirling around you, and you just have to keep your little patch clean somehow. Right?"

"Right," I said. "I know what you mean."

She stared at the blinds I had closed to get it dark enough in the living room. Then she looked back at me.

"And the last line?" I said.

"*Never you mind,*" she quoted in a perfect Texas accent. "*Never you mind.*"

I waited as she thought about it.

"I don't like it," she said.

"Why not?" I said. "It sums up the whole movie! These characters don't have a choice. They just have to put the heartache behind them and move on. Never mind."

"But they should mind!" she said. "Even if it hurts. They should mind. You can't just check out and give up on everything at the age of eighteen. Sonny should have left. Or tried to make things better. I get what it was supposed to mean, but I think it's bullshit. You can't just stop trying because all these forces are against you."

I didn't try to fight her. I had always thought of the line as a survival strategy. You just put the pain out of your mind and find a way to get by. Never you mind. But I didn't want to say that now. As always, Raina's ideas seemed more compelling.

"They're tearing it down no matter what," I said.

Raina was off the couch now, walking over to the window. She pulled open the blinds and the harsh light of the afternoon poured in.

"You're not talking about the movie anymore are you?" she asked.

I shook my head.

"I kind of figured," she said.

I walked over and looked out the window. The sun had dipped behind a thin cloud, giving my boring neighborhood a backlit glow.

"Do you want to call it off?" she said. "I get it if you do."

"No," I said. "*We* can't go out with a whimper."

"Why not?" she said.

"Because then the bad guys win," I said.

36

The two last problems we had to solve for the festival were technical. We had to find a way to show the films even though they would now be digital, and we needed to find a way into the apartment building next door to act as a projection booth. There was, of course, the other problem, which was that we might not get any people or films, but that was out of our control, Raina said. We had to focus on the stuff we could actually do something about.

The first problem was the easiest to solve. Even though Raina was supposed to consult with her mother before making major purchases after she gave away a chunk of her fortune to her father, she bought us a state-of-the-art digital projector and speakers that Anjo helped her to select. She also donated her laptop to the cause because it was the newest of all of ours. The filmmakers could bring their one-minute films on flash drives and load them onto the computer.

Simple enough, we hoped. So, we left Anjo with the manual for the projector and set our sights on the next challenge.

The apartments next door.

And here was the thing with the apartments next door: No one had ever been inside them. Like: ever. And we hardly ever saw anyone coming or going. They were as run-down as the Green Street and twice as old, it seemed. At some point, they had been a long-stay motel, but then they were turned into apartments. As far as we knew, the place was full of ghosts that had just stayed on from the original hotel in the seventies. But time was running short, and there was no choice now but to go in and try to convince someone to let us into their home for the evening. Or else, we all might be watching films the size of a cereal box.

Apartment 3C. That was the unit with the straight shot to the wall. It looked out directly onto the alley and the Green Street. But first we had to get inside. Raina and I stood outside of the building. She looked at the intercom buttons and then reached out a finger. She pressed the one for 3C. There was immediately a sharp buzz and then a crackle from the small speaker.

"Just leave it in the lobby," came a barely audible voice, and then the signal went dead.

Then some silence. I could hear the sound of someone playing the violin off in the distance. Raina and I looked at each other. I pressed the button again.

"Wine delivery, right?" came the voice. "Just leave it in the lobby like last week. I'm watching *The Price Is Right.*"

I pressed the button one more time.

"What part of leave it in the lobby don't you understand?"

"Well," I said, and my voice broke a little. "There was a problem with your order. I . . . uh . . . I need to speak with you about it. Or you'll never get anymore wine. Ever again."

There was a long pause and then a low hum came from the door. I reached out and pushed it open. Raina looked at me, stunned. I shrugged.

The lobby looked worse than the Green Street's. The black-and-white laminate floor was peeling and there was a boarded-up fireplace just inside the doors. We took the old creaky elevator to the third floor and got off in a hallway with green carpet that smelled like it held one-hundred years' worth of cigarette smoke. I swear I saw little clouds puffing out with each step I took. Almost every other building in this area had been taken over by college kids; this one had to be really bad if they hadn't colonized it yet.

"What exactly is your endgame here?" asked Raina right before I knocked.

"We're actors," I said. "Classically trained. We can improvise, right?"

I knocked on the door, and we both listened to the all-encompassing silence. There was no sign of life inside or out. I waited for the sound of creaking floorboards, and for the gruff old guy to open the door so I could warm his cold heart with stories of his neighborhood cinema. But nobody answered. I knocked again, a little louder this time.

"Are you sure you rang the right buzzer," I asked.

"I think so," said Raina.

I looked up at the door. It was definitely 3C. I knocked again, as loud as I possibly could.

"Sir," I yelled. "I am suspending your wine account unless you open up!"

Raina grabbed my arm.

"Hey, easy there!" she said. "Dial it back a notch."

"We need this place!" I said.

I was about to give the door another pummeling, when a different door opened down the hall. And a man wearing boxer shorts, and a full beard came out, looking red-eyed and angry.

"Will you knock it off down there! For God's sake, some people are trying to sleep."

I froze in place. I'm not sure all the acting training in the world could have prepared me to improvise in this situation. The man down the hall was not in his usual clothes, and his beard had grown out a bit since I last saw him, but even in his state of disarray, he wore a relatively clean polo over his boxers.

"Ron?" I said.

His face looked just the way I imagined mine did.

"Wendy," he said.

He turned around as if to go back into his apartment, but I ran down the hallway to him before he could duck inside. He was halfway through the door, and I peered around him at the dim, empty space. Most of his possessions still seemed to be in boxes. There wasn't much furniture. Just a couple of nice suits on hangers in the window.

"Wait a minute. You live here?" I asked.

He turned around. Then he puckered his lips like he was tasting something sour.

"My wife got the house," he said.

"But out of all the other places in town . . ." I said.

"I wanted to keep an eye on my project," he said. "It's kind of all I have going on if you want the truth."

Raina was behind me now, and we were still standing in the hallway. Ron was in his doorway, guarding it now with the bulk of his frame. He seemed to remember, suddenly, how unkempt he was. He ran his fingers through his shaggy beard like a comb.

"Shouldn't you be at work?" I asked.

"I took some time off," he said. "At the request of my employer."

His eyes darted from me to Raina.

"You're that actress," he said. "The one who got arrested."

"Yeah," she said. "That's what we Hollywood elites like to do."

Ron stroked his mustache.

"Why were you bothering Mr. Mulvaney," he asked. "He's almost totally deaf. And a mean drunk. What did you need from that guy?"

I looked down at the green carpeting. Then back into the cave of Ron's apartment.

"Yeah," I said. "About that . . ."

Then, somehow, we were drinking grape soda out of coffee cups with Ron Marsh. When I told him what we needed, he had stared at me for a good twenty seconds before inviting me inside. Now we all sat on boxes. Well, except him. He was planted in a lawn chair with a built-in cup holder. He was currently listening with an inscrutable expression as I told him everything I possibly could about my situation. I told him about my dad, and the film I'd found, and the idea for the festival. I had never explained all of this at once, and the more I told him about my story, the more I realized that my entire life had been defined by the place outside his window.

It was either kind of sad or kind of amazing, depending on how you looked at it. I stood at that window now, staring at the Green Street below me. I had never seen it from this perspective before. It looked so small. And really it was. The projection booth was a hovel. The theater itself only held a couple hundred seats. It was such a tiny place to spend a life in.

"Okay, keep going," said Ron.

I snapped myself from my reverie.

". . . and so our projectionist thinks Mr. Mulvaney's window is the best angle for getting a straight shot at the wall. But, it sounds like he's not going to be so receptive to our plan, so maybe we could make this work . . ."

"This," he said. "As in: my home?"

I stopped and took a sip of my soda, which was quite good. When was the last time I had had grape soda? Ron watched me. I spoke again before he could say no.

"I don't know what else to tell you, Ron, except that you won. The building is being torn down. It's toast. We just want to celebrate it and the people who loved it one last time. And maybe get the community excited about film-making. And if I can show my dad's film, that will feel like something. I'd like to think he'd be happy that a few people saw it. But, obviously I can't make you do anything. And I'm not going to yell at you or make a scene, or stalk you while you're singing karaoke anymore. I'm just going to ask you one time if we can put the projector up here, and then I'll go and you probably won't ever see me again after tonight. I don't know why you would."

I was facing the room now. Raina was on a box to my side, nursing her soda, looking at Ron. Ron was in his lawn chair, his ankles crossed, with squinty eyes. Suddenly, he looked at Raina.

"So, what's the story with you two?" he asked finally.

"What?" I said.

Already, I could feel myself turning red. It was pathetic. Raina looked cool and calm as always.

"Friends," she said. "That's the story."

She didn't look at me. That was her one tell.

"Yeah," I said softly. "Friends."

No one spoke for a moment. Raina immediately filled the silence.

"Is that okay with you?" she said.

Ron chuckled. It was the first time I had seen him smile since we showed up.

"I didn't win," he said suddenly.

"You didn't?" I said.

There was maybe a touch of sarcasm in my voice.

"No," he said. "I didn't. I don't know if the condo project is going to go through. Short-term building loans aren't great right now and . . . well, I don't know if the college is interested anymore. But, that's not really even the point."

"What's the point?" asked Raina.

Her tone was an icy one.

"The point is that my marriage is over. You guys don't care about that, but it took me a long time to come to terms with it. The papers are signed and there's nothing else to be done about it. It's in the past. And I didn't ask about you guys to be a creep, okay? You say that you're friends and that's a nice thing. I don't need details. You care about each other. I can tell. You might even love each other. I just want to tell you that you're lucky. Anyone who has some kind of love in their life is lucky."

Raina and I were quiet.

"That's all. It doesn't always last. Sometimes it's here and gone before you even know it. Sometimes it lasts for years. But you can't take it for granted, okay. That's not fair to people like me."

He got up off his chair and started riffling through a pile of clothes on the floor. I looked over at Raina. Her mouth was closed tight. We both watched him with no idea what to expect. I wouldn't have been surprised if he pulled out a bottle of whiskey or even a gun. Luckily, it was neither. He finally found what he was looking for in the pocket of a pair of jeans.

Keys.

A ring with just a couple on it. He held them out to me. I opened my mouth but he spoke first.

"I'll need them back," he said.

I opened my palm and held it out.

"It's my night to sing. She probably won't be there, but I'm not sure where else to go. You guys can set up your projector. I assume you don't have a permit, so I don't know how long it's going to last, but go ahead and see your place off."

I took the keys.

"Thank you, Ron," I said.

"Don't thank me," he said. "Your building was going to be torn down no matter what—I think that's true—but I probably cost you a couple months. Maybe half a year."

His lips moved to a smile again.

"Or . . ." he said, "I saved you from being inside when it collapsed."

I held the keys in my palm. I swallowed the rest of my soda and got up. Raina was behind me.

"Good luck, you two," he said.

I'm pretty sure he wasn't talking about the festival this time.

Ethan's Glossary of Film Terms

ENTRY #130

INTERMISSION

They don't do these at movies anymore, but
once upon a time there was often a break for
the projectionist to switch reels.

Everyone could go to the bathroom or get some
more popcorn. Sometimes there was a medley of
songs from the movie.

I've only been to one movie with an intermission, and it was weird. That intrusion of
reality takes you out of the dream you were in
before. It allows all those things you weren't
thinking about to pour back in.

Nobody really wants an intermission.
Nobody wants time to think.

37

We had to wait until nightfall to really start everything. There were no houselights outside to turn
down. Just the sun, and it had to turn itself down. We di-
vided up the remaining tasks and split up. Griffin and Lucas
went out scouring campus for stray folding chairs. Anjo set
up the projector in Ron's empty apartment. And Raina and
I sat in the storage room, gathering the last of the untainted
candy. Actually, she was in the corner on her phone, trying
not to look at me, and I was unpacking the Junior Mints.

We hadn't really said much since we left Ron's apartment. I didn't know how to ask her if she cared about what
he said. So, I just tossed rat-chewed boxes of Junior Mints
into a giant garbage bag. I had been at it for twenty minutes
at least when Raina broke the silence.

"Well," she said, "people are talking at least."

I looked up at her.

"About the festival. It's been retweeted a couple hundred times."

"That's good," I said. "Right?"

"Yeah," she said. "The comments aren't necessarily encouraging, though. Here's one that says, 'Who wants to come watch Raina Allen have a nervous breakdown with me tonight?' #brainzap."

I pulled a box of candy out that was totally empty. Not a single mint left, junior or otherwise. It had been drained like a corpse in a vampire movie.

"And here's another one . . ."

She was about to read it then she stopped as her eyes moved over the screen of her phone. I crumpled the empty box and tossed it into the garbage.

"What does it say?" I asked.

Her eyes were a little wide.

"It's not important," she said. "I can't believe people have time to do this all day."

I didn't break my stare. She must have felt it.

"Fine," she said. "It says Raina needs to ditch her loser hometown BF and get with this!"

She turned the phone around to show a picture of a muscle-bound pasty dude in a backward baseball hat and Marines T-shirt.

"Not exactly my type," she said. "But I like his enthusiasm."

"Why are they calling me your boyfriend?" I asked.

"Well," she said, "this probably didn't help."

She tapped her phone a few times and handed it to me. The picture was blurry, but clear enough to see: Raina and I racing away in my car, both grinning like idiots. It was a pretty good action shot. We looked like Bonnie and Clyde, if Bonnie and Clyde were only seventeen and one of them wore a ratty blanket on her head.

"I'm just your partner in crime," I said. "That doesn't mean anything."

"Keep scrolling down," she said.

I did.

"Oh," I said.

There was another grainy picture of us face-to-face in my room. The shade had been pulled, but someone had gotten a shot through the crack between my blinds and the window. It was amazing, actually. If I hadn't felt so exposed, I would have admired the man's craft. We were talking, that's all, but it looked like more.

I was about to say as much when I noticed the headline of the article:

"'I CARE ABOUT HIM MORE THAN ANYONE ELSE. HE'S ALWAYS BEEN THERE FOR ME.' RAINA ALLEN OPENS UP ABOUT THE MYSTERY BOY IN THE PHOTO."

I stopped what I was doing and read the short article. *"He's the only one I want to talk to when things got bad,"* it said. *"He's the reason I came back."*

"Did you actually say all this?" I asked.

"I did," she said. "They were gonna run the photo anyway, so I talked them into letting me say something about it. Who knows what they were going to write?"

She stared down at it, unable to meet my eyes. I'm not sure how much time passed because the next thing I know, she was snapping me back to reality.

"Hey," she said.

"What?"

"Can I have a Junior Mint?"

I tossed her a box. She examined it to see if it was tainted. It didn't seem to be, so she ripped it open, upturned the box, and poured a few directly in her mouth.

"Is it true?" I asked.

"It's true," she said.

I just sat there on a giant box of candy. My thinking place. Only there were a few too many thoughts going through my head at the moment to get a handle on. Like the fact that Raina had told the world how close she felt to me, but I was the last to know. And how this declaration should be enough, but I also couldn't help feeling heartbroken.

"I don't think I would be finishing this film without you, Ethan."

I nodded.

"Seriously," she said. "You actually believe in me."

I opened my own box of candy and ate a handful of mints.

"Can I just ask you a favor?"

She looked at me skeptically.

"Okay," she said.

I looked up at the water-damaged ceiling tiles.

"I'm happy about what you told the paper. And I'm happy you meant it. It means a lot to me."

"Okay," she said again.

"But . . . can you just tell me right now if everything is over again when you leave? I mean, if we're likely to see each other much after that? I think it would be easier if I just knew what was going to happen."

She had her eyes closed again. And I thought it was out of frustration with me, but when she opened them again, she wiped away a tear.

"God . . ." she said. "Ethan."

She took a breath and composed herself.

"What?"

"I don't know," she said. "My mom hates it here. And barring any more meltdowns . . ."

"LA is your home now," I said.

She walked over and sat next me on the box of candy. After a moment, she grabbed my hand and held it tight.

"Okay," I said. "Thanks for telling the truth."

It was warm in the closet and it smelled like chocolate and musty boxes. I was thinking that somehow, even after all the gut-wrenching emotional films I'd seen, movies hadn't quite prepared me for the layers of actual heartbreak. Real-life emotions were weirder. Harder to pin down. I felt a little nauseous, but also hungry. Anxious and calm. I was really aware of my teeth for some reason.

There was no music to tell me the precise moment I was supposed to realize this had all been temporary and it hadn't ended the way I wanted it to.

It was similar when my dad died. I didn't cry when I first heard. Not in that moment. It wasn't until I came back home from school that day and he wasn't on the couch. And I turned on the TV and realized that I hadn't chosen what to watch in months. Maybe years. He always had something on, or something he wanted to show me. And it sounds ridiculous, but I just held the remote and cried because I had no idea what to do with it. He wasn't there anymore to tell me what was what.

I was going to have to figure it out alone.

For now, I was able to take a breath and just continue holding her hand. I reached out an arm to put around her. Only, on the way to her shoulders, my elbow hit another box and it toppled to the ground. And immediately, all of the sadness in the room turned to panic. Raina started screaming. Really loud. It took her a second to form the words that I knew were coming.

"Rat!" she said. "Rat! Oh my God!"

I winced, and looked at the shelf behind me. I didn't see anything moving.

"Dead!" she clarified. "Dead rat!"

I looked down, and sure enough, there was a large dead rat on the ground, surrounded by candy. He had already found his own tomb in the box of Junior Mints, but now I had unearthed him. He was on the floor, curled up like he was sleeping. I nudged him with my shoe just to make sure he wasn't. He didn't move.

"Oh no," I said, and got down on my knees. "Brando."

38

The sun was just starting to set behind the buildings, and we were gathered by the Dumpsters. Raina, Griffin, Lucas, Sweet Lou, and Anjo. They had their heads bowed at my request, and everyone was quiet for the most part. Lucas was typing something on his phone, but he at least had it set to vibrate.

"Someone ancient once said that the enemy of my enemy is my friend," I said. "By that rationale, Brando was a friend of the Green Street. He escaped capture at the hands of our foes. He held down the fort while we were barred from entering it. And, most importantly, he lived and died doing what he loved: eating small bits of corn syrup and chocolate in an enclosed space. We should all be so lucky."

I was holding Brando in a large popcorn bag, suspending him over the Dumpster.

"Rats often get a bad rap. They're kind of ugly. They're

blamed for the bubonic plague, and they ate people's faces off in *Rats: Night of Terror*, a classic film by Bruno Mattei."

"Good movie," said Lucas, looking up from his phone. "Totally didn't see that rat man coming!"

"I know, right?" said Griffin.

"Shut up," said Lou. "Have some respect."

They both clammed up.

"But even though society shuns them," I said, "they're survivors. They have spread all over the world from subways to movie theater storage rooms and they never even dream of giving up! They are our brethren. And Brando . . ."

I held the popcorn bag aloft.

"Brando is our mascot tonight!"

Part of me expected that I might incite some clapping and cheering with this line, but ultimately I was holding a dead rat in a popcorn bag, so nothing like that happened.

My arm was drooping now under his considerable heft.

"So, before we cast him off into the unknown, I would like everyone to drop a ceremonial Milk Dud in his vessel. Who knows what kind of candy they have in the rat afterlife. It's probably not great."

Raina walked around with a box of Milk Duds, looking slightly grossed out. She handed one to each of the Green Street team and then came up and dropped one in the popcorn bag, looking away from the opening as she did so.

"I hereby dedicate the first and last Green Street one-minute Film Festival to Brando the rat. Mascot. Rodent. A creature of appetites and courage."

Each of them slowly came up and deposited their Milk Dud. Then I closed my eyes, loosened my grip, and let the bag drop. Trash day was yesterday, so it had a ways to fall, but it landed soon enough with an echoing thud. All around us the sky was just beginning to turn pink. The streetlights weren't on yet, but it wouldn't be long. There was a row of off-kilter folding chairs, pillaged from a few unlocked class-rooms on campus. The projector sat high in the window of Ron Marsh's bachelor pad along with some speakers, pointed down to the alley below. There was an eerie silence, like the moment in a Western before the town baddies come around the corner for a shoot-out.

We all looked around.

Maybe this is it, I thought. Maybe this is how it ends.

But then a pale man came around the corner and stood at the mouth of the alley. He was wearing the skinniest jeans I had ever seen, with a big bob of hair on his head. Most of his face was pierced, and it took me a moment to recognize him from Box Office Video. I had only ever seen him seated behind the counter. It was odd to see him with legs. He just looked at us for a minute, all surrounding an industrial-size Dumpster. Then he looked behind him to see if he was in the right place.

"So," he said. "Is this the festival thing?"

No one spoke for a moment. Finally he met eyes with Raina. She looked as surprised as anyone.

"Yeah," she said.

The clerk riffled in his pocket and pulled out a small green thing.

A flash drive.

"Okay, good," he said. "I brought a movie."

ETHAN'S GLOSSARY OF FILM TERMS

ENTRY #152

DAY FOR NIGHT

A trick directors use to film a nighttime scene
in the day. It used to be hard to get enough
light to shoot at night, so they faked it.

I've always liked the way it looks in old
movies. Like the moonlight is enough to
light up the whole world.

Like a single night holds all the promise of
a new day.

39

An hour later, the alley was starting to fill up. They showed up in clusters, sticking mostly to their own kind. Fans with film stills of Raina, hoping for autographs. Regulars from the Green Street. Fanboys and movie geeks. There was even someone who claimed to be a reporter from the *Tribune*. By the time it was dark, there were probably fifty people and about twenty total folding chairs. It was pitch-black in the alley except for the white glow of the projection on the brick wall. There were two hours until Raina left for the airport.

Anjo was up in Ron's apartment, prescreening the videos to make sure there was no porn. There were about fifteen movies total. When I looked up at her in the dimly lit window, she gave me a hesitant thumbs-up. Griffin was in the crowd, handing out free candy, and occasionally administering one of his drops. Lucas was standing in the crowd, transfixed by the spectacle. And Sweet Lou was our lookout. In case of the police, she was going to sound an air horn. She stood at the end of the alley like a sentry.

It was finally dark enough to get a good picture on the makeshift wall screen, so I threaded my way to the front of the crowd and tried to announce the beginning of the festival. The noise from the crowd was loud though, and no one was really listening. I cleared my throat two different times and even let out a pretty loud whistle, but nobody paid any attention.

Finally, I heard the racket die down all at once. Like someone had waved a wand. I looked to my right and found Raina standing beside me. All it took was her presence to bring everyone to silence. She looked at me expectantly, and I leaned over and whispered in her ear.

"I think they came to see you," I said. "You better say something first."

She nodded.

"Hello, Minneapolis," she said. "Hi, everybody."

A whole group of people at the back cheered like they were at a concert,

"Wooooooooooooooooo! *Time Zap!*" someone yelled.

"Wow, okay," she said. "Yeah. I was in that."

"We love you!" said someone else.

"I'm sure I would love you, too, if I got to know you," she said.

She was smiling now, and it felt to me like her transformation was complete. She was Raina Allen, young celebrity again. All it took was a few fans to switch the light back on.

She pretended she didn't like the attention, but it had to be thrilling some of the time. Especially, if you'd just decided to be that person again.

"I'm Raina," she said. "But this isn't really my event. It's my friend Ethan's. So I'm going to turn things over to him in just a minute. I just want to say that it's possible I wouldn't be an actress if I didn't come here to see movies, and I wish it could live on forever. But, I'm excited to see your movies tonight. I'm sure they're going to be great. Ethan?"

She turned toward me, and I couldn't help flinching. I assumed she was going to speak for longer, maybe even give a rousing speech. But she just pointed at me. I looked at the crowd of people, many of them I had never seen before. Probably most of them had never seen a movie here. Or if they had, it was only once with their weird friend. I didn't resent them—not much anyway—but I wished I could have found a way to get them here sooner.

"Okay, everyone," I said.

I tried to project my voice the way Mrs. Salazar had taught us at the Playhouse.

"Thanks for coming."

It was so quiet now, and I felt my nerves suddenly. Heat in my armpits. A tickle in my throat. I wasn't used to talking to this many people. The only thing that helped was that most of the people were still staring at Raina, not me. I looked around for some familiar faces in the crowd, and eventually, I spotted Griffin, the screen reflecting in his giant glasses. Lucas was at the fringes of the crowd, watching too. Up above me, Anjo was looking down as usual, a benevolent god we did not deserve. And Sweet Lou was at the very end of the alley, holding her air horn with her arm in a sling.

"Home," I said.

It felt good to say the word out loud.

"This place is home. I grew up here. My dad, who isn't here anymore, used to take me here when I was a kid, and I thought it was the single greatest place on the planet. It just felt good being here with him. The old seats that swallow you when you sit down. The noisy house projector. The crackle of the old speaker system. Movies were my dad's religion and I guess I was an easy convert. I told myself that his temple was going to be here forever, which is probably also what I thought about him."

I took a breath and tried to stand up straight. There were some befuddled looks from the crowd now. This was supposed to be a party.

"They're going to knock it down now, and they might or might not make some stylish places for young people to live. I tried to fight it. But in the end there wasn't much I could really do. You can't save everything, no matter how much you might care about it. In the end, your love can't keep it alive."

I glanced at Raina, and though she was smiling for the crowd, she gave me a concerned look.

"But there might have been one thing I was wrong about."

I turned around to look at it for a moment. Then I turned back.

"I thought the building was everything. I don't think I was right about that. It might not be the space itself. It might be the people who came to the building. My fellow employees, the regulars, anyone else who showed up to be part of it. All the people who kept it going for as long as they could. And so, I guess what I want to say is that if you have a good time tonight, just think about finding more ways to do this. It doesn't have to be here. Just find ways to be together to do something you really care about. If you can make art together and find your people, maybe that's enough."

No one said anything. The alley was totally quiet.

"Can we?" I said, motioning to Anjo. "Can we just maybe roll the first film?"

She nodded and began clicking on the laptop.

"The rest of the night is for you," I said. "It's yours."

I walked away then, through the crowd and around the corner. I left the alley, and walked back into the lobby of the apartment complex. I rode the elevator back up to the third floor. Then I walked down to 3F, Ron's apartment, where I helped myself to a grape soda from the fridge and stood next to Anjo at the projector. The first film had already started playing. Anjo adjusted the focus, and everything that was fuzzy at the edges, suddenly became perfectly clear.

40

I can't lie. The first couple of films were pretty bad. The first one was just a guy following his girlfriend around, filming her in the most flattering light possible, When it was over, people clapped politely, more because the festival had started than because they thought he was a cinematic genius. The second one was about a dog in love with another dog at the park. It was kind of cute, I guess.

Down below, Raina sat in the front row, taking her judging duties seriously. She smiled and signed the occasional autograph between movies. Anjo seemed to be enjoying her role, loading up each film, one after the next, allowing for a little transition time between each. All the equipment worked surprisingly well. The picture was sharp. The speakers were loud enough, even if the sound echoed a bit in the alley. And the view out of the window was pretty spectacular. You could see about a four-block swathe from where we were, and in the middle of it, we'd turned a dingy ally into an outdoor theater.

"I'm pretty sure he would have liked this, Ethan," said Anjo after the dog film ended.

I knew immediately who she was talking about, but it surprised me. She didn't mention my dad all that often.

"I hope so," I said.

"Of course he would have," she said. "The Cinema of Revolt! What's more punk rock than a DIY movie festival? It's illegal. We're celebrating guerrilla filmmaking! The art of the people."

"And dog movies," I said.

"And dog movies," she said, and smiled. "You should keep an open mind. The quality might pick up."

I looked down.

"I hope so, for Raina's sake."

There was more polite clapping from below. Anjo located the next file and clicked it. A shot came on of someone running through a yard, carrying a knife. Bad sound effects of sirens were layered over the action. It was a college frat-boy thriller. An early Christopher Nolan rip-off.

"I was kind of in love with him, you know," said Anjo.

I turned away from the movie.

"My *dad*?"

She was still watching the wall below.

"It's probably not something you want to hear, but I don't know how much we'll see each other after tonight, so I feel like I have to tell you."

"Okay . . ." I said.

Somehow, I wasn't that shocked. More curious than anything else.

"But why? He was a middle-aged professor."

"You of all people should know why. You loved him, too."

"He was my dad."

"Well," she said, "I didn't really know my dad very well. And I saw him more than either of my parents. So, he was kind of my dad, too. Except that I wanted to be married to him."

"Oh," I said. "Well, I'm glad it wasn't weird or anything."

I expected Anjo to laugh. But she didn't. She just looked at me.

"He found his exact place in the world," she said. "How many people get to do that? I mean, sure he wasn't the pope or the president. He was a professor at a state university and the guardian of a campus movie theater. But this is exactly where he fit. It was like the universe picked him up and set him down here. And that's an intoxicating thing."

"I know," I said.

"It makes you feel like it's possible for anyone. Like, if this guy can find his thing, then why can't you or I find our thing? The only trouble is that it's pretty easy to mistake his passion for your own. Sometimes, I wonder if I stayed here so long because he made such a convincing argument for all of it. The power of film. That Art House theater. He made it seem like the best place to be. The only place to be. But, I haven't really traveled much. I barely left the projection booth the last ten years."

"Are you trying to tell me all this is a good thing? The fact that we don't know what's happening next or what the hell we're going to do with our lives?"

She sighed and adjusted her glasses.

"I don't know if I completely believe that. I probably could have been happy in that booth for a few more years. Maybe longer. Look at Lou. She's a lifer and there was probably nothing else she wanted to do. I guess my point is that I don't know. But, what if I haven't totally found my thing yet. What if my thing is in Olympia, Washington? Or Helsinki? Or in Saint Paul? Or what if I don't have a thing. What if I have like ten things instead? Maybe I have five destinies and this is only the first one."

The frat-boy thriller came to a predictable blood-spattered end, which was a favorite with the crowd below. They laughed and applauded the blast of watered-down ketchup that exploded onto the screen.

"Well," she said. "Actually, I might be too old for five destinies at this point. I could probably fit in three. But you, Ethan! You're not even eighteen. You probably have time for seven or eight destinies. It's kind of narrow to count on one, don't you think?"

I was looking down at Raina now. I couldn't help it. All this talk of destiny, and my eyes could only go one place. It was bad enough the Green Street was done, but it was nearly impossible to picture a life where Raina and I weren't together. In my mind, it had always been a given. I wasn't sure how long it was going to take, but I had always planned to wait it out. In my mind, it had always been a *when* not an *if*. *When she finally realizes nobody knows her like me. When she gets tired of living in LA. When I get a little better looking and take over the Green Street.*

The crazy thing is that it had all almost happened. I had come really close. She came back. She missed me. She slept in my bed wearing my T-shirt. But there was no almost-destiny. I could try to frame it any way I wanted, but it just didn't happen.

"Will you allow me one last Steve McQueen anecdote while I'm still technically the projectionist?" Anjo said.

"Is there any reality where you don't tell me this story?" I asked.

"Probably not," she said.

"Okay," I said. "Then go ahead."

She clicked open the next film. This one was just someone dancing in the city. Doing flips off bus stops. Swinging around signs. Like a modern-day Fred Astaire. It was kind of entrancing.

"Do you know what Terrence's first leading role was?" she asked.

I thought for a moment. I had definitely looked up

McQueen's filmography when I first met Anjo.

"Wait a minute, it wasn't . . ."

"*The Blob*," she said.

"Whoa," I said.

"Yeah," she said. "The future King of Cool starred in a movie about a giant space amoeba that eats people in Pennsylvania. It was a questionable career choice. But beyond that, something interesting happened with his contract. When he signed on to star in the film, McQueen had the choice to take a flat fee of six thousand dollars or a smaller salary with a percentage of the profits. He thought the movie was ridiculous, and he was broke, so he took his flat fee and was happy to do it. I imagine it probably seemed like a safe bet at the time. It was a B movie. Take your money and run, Terrence! Only, as we now know, *The Blob* was a huge hit. It was improbable. Critics hated it, but horror fans loved it. And if only Terrence had taken the other deal, do you know how much he would have made?"

"I don't," I said.

"Around a million dollars. And this is in 1958."

I whistled. It seemed the only appropriate response.

"He never took a flat fee again. He always rolled the dice, even late in his career when he could demand enormous salaries."

Below us, the experimental dance film came to a stop with a finale in a fountain. It wasn't bad, actually. The editing was pretty impressive for something done on a laptop. And the acrobatic dancing was cool.

"Anjo," I said, "I know I'm not supposed to ask the Oracle what her advice and prophesies mean. That's kind of the point. But I'm just too tired to try to figure this one out right now. I assume it doesn't have to do with money because we don't have any. And I don't plan on being an actor anytime soon."

Anjo paused for a second to load the next film.

I looked down when she was done. The film was one I recognized. A pair of shoes walking down the street, ready to find their way to the Green Street. I looked at Anjo.

"I had it digitally transferred," she said. "Now it has played in one festival."

I felt the urge to be back down with the crowd suddenly, to be crammed in the alley, seeing it like they were. I turned to go, but before I could make my exit, Anjo touched me on the shoulder. When I turned around, she placed something in my hand. It was the flash drive of Dad's film. I closed my hand around it, and gave her a hug. I felt the urge to run down the stairs, so I wouldn't miss too much of the movie.

"Ethan," she said.

"What?"

"Our lives might be *The Blob*. Or they might not. I just don't know. But I think we have to gamble."

I smiled.

I was halfway out the door when I heard the air horn.

ETHAN'S GLOSSARY OF FILM TERMS

ENTRY #96

PERSISTENCE OF VISION

This is a famous theory about how film works
with our eyes. The fact that we can watch
twenty-four still frames per second and it
looks like it's moving.

Supposedly, it works because the human eye
holds an image for just a little longer than
it's actually there. So, we're always seeing a
little bit of the past even as we're looking
at the present.

It's only a fraction of a second, but the idea
is comforting to me. Our eyes want to hold
on to the past, even when we're trying to see
what happens next.

41

By the time I got down to the street, my dad's movie was almost over. And most of the audience was still watching it even though a small argument had broken out at that mouth of the alley. I moved through the crowd slowly, carving a path through the filmgoers. At first I could barely see what was going on. There was a campus security car parked at the end of the road and a few shadows, but it was tough to tell what was really happening. When I made it out the other side, I found Lucas waiting for me.

"It's not the real cops," he said. "But the security guy's being a total dong."

We both approached the altercation. As I got closer, I noticed it was the same security guard who had been in the president's office trying to get Griffin expelled. He had a flashlight pointed directly at Lou, and he was trying to move forward, but she was holding on to the sleeve of his uniform. He was a little on the lanky side, and when he flapped his arm, he looked like a tall, flightless bird. But he finally shook her loose.

"You can't go in there without a ticket," she said. "It's a sold-out event."

"Will you please stop talking," said the guard. "You're giving me a headache."

He had just taken a couple of steps forward when he came face-to-face with Lucas and me. He recognized me instantly, and let out a long, slow breath.

"Why are you harassing an elderly woman?" I asked.

"Because he's on a sad little power trip" said Lou, "And he has nothing better to do."

He looked back at Lou only enough to shoot her a scowl. Then he opened his eyes wide and searched the alley.

"You know you're not supposed to be doing this," he said, and looked toward the screen. "Whatever this is."

His face looked a little ashen. I turned around and saw the video clerk on the screen in close up. He was slowly filling his mouth with marbles, seeing how many could fit. The more he stuffed in, the more fell out. It was, in all fairness, pretty disturbing.

"It's a film festival," said Lucas. "Some of the work is quite avant-garde. Like this piece here that echoes some of the early conceptual work of William Wegman."

The marbles were all bouncing out now as the clerk stared into the camera.

"Yeah," said the guard. "I'm shutting this down. You can't be blocking traffic in the alley. This is a liability for the university."

"No one uses this alley," I said.

But he swiftly moved around Lucas and me and headed toward the crowd, looking up to see where the films were coming from. He had his flashlight on, and the viewers were starting to look at him instead of the screen.

"Wait. We can't be done yet," Lucas said suddenly.

Even the guard stopped for a second. Lucas's plea was so raw and genuine. There was something a little desperate in his voice that I had never heard before. In fact, it had been a really long time since I heard something that wasn't either ironic or condescending from him.

"Why not?" I asked, though I had plenty of my own reasons why we shouldn't be done.

"They haven't shown my film yet!" he said.

"You actually made a film?" I asked.

Lucas nodded, a sheepish smile on his face. The guard had had enough, but when he tried to enter the crowd, no one made space for him. He clicked on his flashlight and started shining it at people. Some folks averted their eyes, but nobody really moved.

"Campus security," he said. "Get out of the way."

There were some groans of mild protest.

He began muscling his way into the group, nudging people aside. It wasn't very elegant. I could tell he wasn't really a master of crowd control. In fact, he looked so uncomfortable and flustered, I almost felt bad for him. That is, until he collided with the guest of honor.

He was pushing his way toward the front, and when he was almost there, he tripped over the leg of a folding chair and fell across a sparse row of them, finally barreling into Raina. She had been watching from her seat as all of this went down, but she wasn't expecting the contact. It knocked her over, and she landed flat on her back in the alley.

The gasp that went through the crowd was almost simultaneous. Everyone saw her fall. Everyone stared at the guard in disbelief. Had he really just harmed a celebrity? Could he do that? Somebody reached down to help Raina up, and she seemed okay. But the crowd had already turned. The guard got up to see if Raina was all right, and a large goth guy in a Batman T-shirt stepped forward and blocked his path. But before goth Bruce Wayne could do anything, Raina was back in the mix.

She looked unnaturally calm as she approached the guard. I thought she'd be angrier after her fall, but it looked like she just wanted to talk. Just when she had reached him and opened her mouth to say something, the crowd lurched forward. Someone must have pushed from the back, but Raina, the goth guy, and everyone near the officer moved in a wave, gradually pushing the bewildered officer outside the circle of viewers.

"Hey," said Raina. "Knock it off!"

But it was too late.

There were a few other guards on the scene, checking to see what was going on. One of them asked who these "weirdos" were and was promptly pelted with a box of Sour Patch kids, to a roar of approval from the crowd. Another guard reached for his pepper spray and that's pretty much when all hell broke loose. Someone ran toward the guard, knocking the spray out of his hand. Others ran away. Candy soared through the air. It was almost like a Parisian riot.

Almost.

I covered my head and charted a path to Raina. As I waded through the fray, I was hit with at least two Milk Duds and a cup of something that might have been Sprite. Soon the wail of actual police sirens went up and people started fleeing for real. The guards chased them through the alleys, dodging candy boxes and insults. It all happened so fast, it was shocking when the alley was nearly clear. There were a few hangers-on watching from behind the Dumpsters, but everyone else was pursued or pursuing somewhere on the civilian streets of campus. Which left Raina and me in the first row of folding chairs, the white light of the projector shining in our eyes.

"Are you okay?" I asked.

She nodded.

"That happened fast," she said. "I never got to pick a winner."

"Eh," I said. "Winning things is overrated."

She gave me a skeptical look.

"Think about it. When you win, you don't get to be an underdog anymore. What happens at the end of every movie where the good guys win? They all smile and congratulate themselves and then the story is over. There's nothing left to do except sit around feeling good about yourself forever, or until someone dreams up a sequel. Who wants to do that? At least when you lose, you still have something to care about."

We both looked up to a stray festival-goer running down the alley with his shirt off screaming. I waited for him to stop and talk to us, but he just kept going.

"Ethan," Raina said when he passed. "I know this has got to be hard for you."

"Not really," I said. "Everything's fine. I'll be fine."

"No you won't," she said.

I wasn't expecting that answer, but she didn't qualify it.

"What the hell kind of thing is that to say?" I asked.

"The truth," she said.

She got out her phone, and I watched as she looked up the number for Yellow Cab. But while she dialed, she still looked me in the eyes.

"I know what it's like to lose the thing you care about most. It feels like you've lost your center of gravity. Like you've suddenly come loose and there's nothing to hold you down. So, I'm not going to tell you that you're going to wake up tomorrow and everything is going to be fine. It's just not true. But lucky for you, I know what helps."

She paused for a second to order her cab, slowly explaining to the dispatcher where she was and where she needed to go. When she was done, she opened something else on her phone. She kept tapping and I waited patiently for her to finish her thought. But she wasn't looking up.

"What are you doing?" I asked.

She handed me her phone and then started walking out of the alley. I stumbled behind her, looking down at the screen. It was an airline company. It was a flight reservation for me. To LA.

"It's already paid for," she said.

"But . . ."

"I got some info from your mom," she said. "You leave in a month."

I stared down at the flight information. I had a seat number. It was real.

I followed Raina out of the alley, looking up at the window of the apartment building as I went. Anjo was no longer there. Just the light, and the rectangle on the wall. The police sirens were getting closer.

I walked out onto the street, where Raina watched in the distance for her cab, unbothered by the potential of more police.

"But won't you be in Greenland or something?"

"Filming starts in LA. They're doing the first part on a soundstage. Movies aren't real, remember, Ethan?"

"Raina . . ." I said.

"Just take it," she said. "Take the flight in a month."

I heard her voice give a little, and I could see that her decisive attitude was just a facade.

"It's not just for you," she said.

Down the street, I saw the hint of a yellow cab pointed in our direction. It pulled over, and the driver rolled down his window. Raina smiled at the driver and held up her hand, then she looked at me.

"Either you come see me or I stay here now," she said. "Your choice."

I laughed. I couldn't help it.

"What?" she said.

"You can't stay," I said.

"Why not?" she said.

"I can't believe I have to explain this to you," I said.

The cabdriver looked back at Raina, impatient. She didn't seem to notice. She was still looking at me. I tried to smile.

"If you stay," I said, "then the bad guys win."

She smiled back. Then I handed the phone to her. Raina finally moved toward the cab and opened the door. I briefly wondered how many emotional good-byes this driver had seen. How many times he was forced to wait as the show went on as if he didn't exist.

"I've never flown anywhere by myself," I said.

Raina gave me a frustrated look I recognized from another time.

"You go to the airport and get on a plane, Ethan. C'mon, I can't hold your hand forever."

She sat down in the taxi then and I reached out to close the door. But before I could, she stood up and gave me a hug.

"Thank you," she said.

She held me tight, her arms like a vise against my back.

"For what?" I said.

She smiled.

"For helping me out. For distracting me. For being my friend again, even if I didn't really deserve it."

"I'll always be your friend," I said.

She nodded.

"I love you, Ethan," she said.

"I love you, too," I said.

She let go of me. Then she gave me one last look, and closed the door. I watched the cab drift down the street, finally disappearing around a corner. There wasn't much traffic then, and even though I knew I shouldn't, I walked back to the alley to see what was left.

The light from the projector had gone out, and there was only a single policeman looking at the folding chairs, trying to make sense of what had happened. He looked up at me when I entered, and I was sure he was going to come over and slap a pair of cuffs on me. But of course, he had no idea who I was or that I had even been there. He looked confused more than alarmed. He picked up a box of candy and shook it.

"Do you know what this was all about?" he asked.

I didn't know what to say, so I did what I always do when I don't know what to say: I quoted a movie.

"Never you mind," I said. "Never you mind."

42

We all met on Washington Street.

Three weeks had passed and we stood behind the green plastic fence covered in Caution signs. Lou, Griffin, Lucas, Anjo, and I. It was one of those early fall days where the sky just seems to get bluer the longer you look at it. There were no clouds. Not even a bird. And underneath it all, a tiny movie theater stood in the shadow of a towering red crane with a wrecking ball attached to the end. For now, the ball was motionless, just hanging there like a moon in orbit.

It was eight a.m. and in the last week, the weather had turned cool. All of us had coffee, steam curling out from the little escape hatches in our to-go cups. Lou had a new electric wheelchair and she had taken it through a drive-through and come bearing the five cups in her basket. She doled them out with a calm efficiency.

"Is there any cream?" Griffin had asked.

Lou shook her head.

"'Fraid not," she said. "Today we drink it black. Like our souls."

No one complained.

In the last few weeks, we had all kept in touch by text, brainstorming ideas about what we could do when this was all over. Anjo suggested a nonprofit Film Arts organization. Lucas thought we should stage more pop-up cinemas. Maybe on the walls of multiplexes. Show them what real movies were. Griffin was still spouting conspiracy theories about Ron March, and Lou mostly sent dirty jokes. Out of all of us, she seemed to be enjoying her forced retirement the most.

As of yet, no real plan of action had been decided. There were times when I made myself get excited about what this crew could do next, but now that we were all standing together here in the light of day, it felt like those texts had just been late-night ideas. Waking dreams born of desperation. The truth was that we were all probably going to move on with our lives in some way or another.

Anjo and I had talked just a few days ago. She was thinking of teaching English abroad. Seeking her second destiny.

"I've always liked Czech films," she'd said. "Maybe I'll go to Prague."

I'd been sitting in the backyard at the time, taking in

some rare sunlight on my skin. It wasn't the worst feeling in the world, I had to admit. It was possible I could get used to this being outside thing. In small doses at least.

"What am I supposed to do without an oracle?" I asked.

"Haven't you read the Greeks?" she said. "No one listens to oracles anyway. We all make our mistakes no matter what."

It was silent on the line for a moment.

"I'll leave you my e-mail," she said. "There's no reason oracles have to meet face-to-face these days."

She hadn't told the others her plans, but she didn't say much today as we watched the scene in front of us. She just took small sips of piping hot coffee like the rest of us.

"I think it's moving," said Griffin.

It was the first thing anyone had said in a while.

"No it's not," Lucas said. "You're moving."

Which was true. Griffin was swaying side to side in a little melancholy shuffle.

"Those options aren't mutually exclusive," said Griffin.

Which was also true. Because now the crane really was moving.

The demolition had been slated for eight fifteen, and here they were starting right on time. I'm not sure we ever started a movie on time during my entire tenure at the Green Street. But on its last day, there would finally be punctuality. The neck of the crane moved back and forth until the ball built some momentum. Then, when it was really swinging, the line dropped and the wrecking ball went crashing through the top of the gray brick facade, sending a storm of century-old bricks raining down on the ground below.

We all watched in silence.

The crane jerked again, and the ball met the top story head-on, bursting through in a giant hole. Everyone looked at Anjo. It was clear that her former home had just been trashed. I put a hand on her shoulder, but she didn't tense. She just wiped the lenses of her glasses for a better look.

"I thought it would be louder," she said.

"Or more explosive," said Griffin.

"These assholes can't do anything right," said Lou.

We watched as a few more strategic hits sent the right side cascading down in a slow avalanche of old cement, wood, and Sheetrock. The dust cloud was impressive, like the aftermath of a small bomb. A few students stopped to watch, taking videos with their phones, then scurrying along to class. A cyclist buzzed behind us, cursing the protective fences that kept him from his usual route. Everything was crashing down, but life went on as usual.

"Whoa," said Griffin. "Check it out. The marquee's still up."

He was right. Despite all the other damage, it still stood perfectly straight, like a flag still planted in the soil.

How many times had I climbed up a ladder, a slight

sense of vertigo kicking in, to change the letters of whatever feature was coming soon? How many times had Griffin or Lucas added a joke in poor taste beneath the title that Randy made us take down? It must have been something in its day. Full of blinking lights and neon. It hadn't lit up properly in years, yet it stood to the last, clutching on to the remains of the building, avoiding the crane like a squirrelly kid in gym class, waiting out a game of dodgeball.

"Hey," I said. "Let's go, guys."

"What?" said Lucas.

Everyone else turned toward me.

"If we leave now, we never see the marquee go down. Look at it."

We all stared.

"If we go right this minute, then it's still standing. In our minds, I mean."

"I don't know," said Griffin.

"Wendy's right," said Lucas. "We don't need to see it. Let's let it live."

Lou shrugged and turned her wheelchair around so she was facing away. Then Anjo turned, too. It was only a matter of moments until the ball made contact with it. But it hadn't happened yet. Slowly, Lucas and Griffin turned around. I took one last look and turned the other way, too.

"What happens to the Lost Boys at the end of *Peter Pan*?" said Griffin. "I don't remember."

"They leave Neverland," I said. "They grow up."

"I was afraid you were going to say that," said Griffin.

"It's not as bad as it sounds," said Lou.

"How so?" said Anjo.

She seemed genuinely interested.

"I don't know," said Lou, smiling now. "You meet some interesting people."

From behind us came the loudest crash yet, like the sound of an entire structure collapsing. I wanted so badly to see if the marquee had come down, but so far everyone else was holding strong. I thought maybe if I took one step, I could walk away clean, keep moving forward. I closed my eyes and tried one. It was a little easier to breathe. I took one more, and soon I was walking. I heard a few footsteps behind me. I had no idea if I was walking forward, but at least I wasn't looking back.

ETHAN'S GLOSSARY OF FILM TERMS
ENTRY #999

FADE-OUT

The last image slowly fades away. Then there's black.

If it's done well, it leaves you breathless. Sometimes it's just a relief. Most of the time it's somewhere in the middle.

No matter what it always makes me a little sad, though. It's like a Sunday night with school the next day. You know the credits are going to start rolling soon. And after the credits, you have to walk out of the theater.

Then there's life again, waiting for you.

It hasn't gone anywhere. Your quick plunge into another existence is over.

What used to make me feel better was knowing Dad and I would have a conversation afterward. We'd keep the feeling going by talking through what we'd seen.

Now it's up to me. The lights are on again. It's my choice if it's an ending or a beginning.

AFTER THE CREDITS

I f I was in a movie, I would be on this plane to start a new life.

People only buy one-way tickets in movies.

There are no return flights. No one ever goes back to who they were. Sometimes I think this is true. Other times I don't. I'll save you the drama and tell you right off that I have a return ticket. I'm not moving to Los Angeles. I'm coming back to Minnesota in a week. Still, I suppose my old life is over whether I like it or not. Whatever comes next, good or bad, can never be what it was before.

Mom and I went to see my dad's grave this morning before we left for the airport. It's been a year since I was last there. I don't feel like I really need to go there to think about him, but Mom wanted to visit, and she's letting me jet off to LA unsupervised, so I said okay, and we took a drive to the place just outside of town where we buried him three years ago.

We didn't bring flowers.

He never liked them in life, so why would he like them now? Mom brought food. It was for us, but she thought he might like to be in close proximity of her cooking. It was one of her regrets that she only became a good chef once he was gone. I brought him an article about the destruction of the Green Street, and another copy of his film that I made on my computer. When we got there, it took a while to get to his plot. It's out in the latest part of the development, near some young trees that will someday be tall and old. He's on top of a hill, and you can see a lot from up there. The duck pond. Some weeping willows. And even a stretch of highway heading back to town.

We were quiet on the way out, but when we got there, Mom started talking as we hoofed it over the gravel path to his spot.

"No tattoos," she said.

I looked around the empty cemetery, and then back at Mom.

"When you're in LA," she said. "I don't want you coming back with any tattoos. Or face piercings. And don't do any adult films, even if someone offers you a lot of money."

"Mom," I said. "Believe me. I am not qualified to work in adult films. In any way."

"You never know. People go out there, and all kinds of crazy things happen. This girl I went to college with was on one episode of a soap opera and then she got addicted to Quaaludes."

"I don't think anyone takes those anymore."

She was walking briskly, holding on to a Tupperware container of eggplant and cashew salad with fresh basil. I'd spent most of the morning helping her prepare it, and I even managed a decent chiffonade on the basil, which earned an impressed smile. Now she had the container tucked under her arm like a football. I was barely keeping up with her when she came to a stop.

"Okay," she said, squinting into the sun. "I'm sorry, but I'm allowed to worry. I don't have your dad anymore, and so if you go out there and get caught up in something, I'll be all alone. And that is not a possibility I'm willing to think about."

"I'm not staying, Mom. And I promise I won't get involved in erotic films or Quaaludes."

She took a few deep breaths. She got allergies this time of year, and her eyes were a little red. Dad's grave was in sight now, and she peered over at it before looking back at me.

"Your dad always said I should leave you alone more often. That you'd find your way. Did you know that?"

I shook my head.

"He told me you were smart and you weren't boring. So you'd find something interesting to do with your life. It might take a little while, but eventually you'd find your thing. He wasn't worried."

"Well," I said, "things haven't been boring. He was right about that, I guess."

"He was right about a lot of things," she said.

We both walked to the foot of the hill and looked up. His stone was at the top, in a row with a few others. Some of them were already there when he died. There were a couple new additions.

"But not everything," she said.

I looked up at the stone.

"What do you mean?" I asked.

"He thought he'd have time to do it all, Ethan. Every little thing he wanted to do. Go on a trip to Europe to see all the locations in his favorite foreign films. Write one more book. Take some filmmaking classes. He was sure he'd have time to make it all happen. It was another thing he never doubted."

She opened the container of salad and plucked a piece of cubed eggplant off the top. She put it in her mouth and chewed.

"But we don't have all the time in the world," she said.

She put a hand on the back of my neck. Then she walked up the hill and made us a picnic by Dad's spot. We ate some salad and sat in the cool air and the warm sun. I wasn't in the habit of talking to graves, so I just left Dad his gifts in a moment by myself, and then I made my way to the car, so Mom could drive me to the airport. Before she dropped me off with my new rolling suitcase, we sat there looking at the place.

"I can't remember the last time I left here," I said.

"It's been a while," she said. "You were married to that theater."

I nodded.

"It was my place," I said.

She looked at me, and then stared out the windshield at the planes taking off. Then she laughed.

"What?" I said.

"People get more than one," she said. "You know that, right?"

I smiled in spite of myself.

"I guess," I said.

It was time to get out of the car. I only had an hour or so to make it through security. Mom walked around and got my suitcase for me. Then she made sure I had my boarding pass. I hugged her, and even though I was coming back soon, I could tell this was just the practice round. Soon enough I'd probably be headed somewhere else, and probably for longer than a week.

I felt my phone buzz in my pocket, but I waited to look at it until I was stuck in the security line.

"I'm taking you hiking," it said.

There was a picture of a trail that went right below the Hollywood sign. Raina's arm was in the shot, flexing into a muscle.

"Hmmm," I wrote back. "Is there an indoor version?"

There was no response for a moment. I expected an

ironic "ha-ha," maybe a frowning emoji at my subpar joke. Instead I got: **"I've really missed you."**

I looked at the words.

We had been texting a lot since she left, more than I expected. And for the last few nights, she had been counting down the days until my arrival. Texting me nothing but the number before she went to bed. 5, 4, 3, 2, 1. And now predictably, a zero came through, enclosed in its little text bubble.

"0"

I closed my eyes a moment then opened them again.

"I've missed you too," I wrote.

The line in front of me was moving faster now. A family up ahead was fumbling with their devices, emptying their pockets of all the little things they carried around to make it through a day. Soon it would be my turn.

"It's weird," she wrote, **"but I feel kind of nervous."**

It was like she read my mind. My heart slowed just to hear her acknowledge it.

"Why?" I wrote. **"It's just me."**

There was no response.

"Maybe this whole 'hiking' thing is too much pressure," I said. **"We should probably do something more low-key like eat tacos in a dark room."**

I was just filling space. Typing to keep the message going. I was almost to the front of the line.

"Don't say it like that," she wrote.

"Say what like what?"

"Just you."

"But it is just me."

Another pause. I stood in front of a conveyer belt. It wanted to swallow my phone. I pulled off my shoes and then looked down at the screen one last time.

"That's enough," it said.

I read the words a couple times. Then I darkened the screen and tossed the phone in a bin. I watched it roll down the conveyer.

An hour disappeared and the next thing I knew, I was stuck in this seat. I was a little uneasy at first. I hadn't been on a plane in a few years. Luckily, I remembered my computer. I opened it up and stared at a file on my desktop. A week after the demolition, Lucas had sent everyone a huge zip file. It was all his footage from the Green Street edited into eight individual episodes. The file was called: *This Film Is Not Yet Rated.*

In the last few weeks, I had fallen behind on my film viewing. It was a four-hour flight, and this would probably get me all the way there. The plane was moving now, and I was about to hit play, when suddenly my finger stopped in midair. It must have looked kind of silly, but I couldn't press play. Instead I closed my laptop. Maybe I'd watch it later if I got bored. For now, I looked out the window as the plane picked up speed. I tried to focus on the world blurring past.

ACKNOWLEDGMENTS

Once upon a time, in an uncertain world without Netflix, I had a job at a little campus movie theater in Minneapolis called the Oak Street Cinema. We showed indie films, classics, foreign films, and the occasional trashy horror flick. It was a beautiful little community of nerds and weirdos and if I had never been a part of it, I would not have written this book. Sadly, it no longer exists, but my treasured memories of stale Dots and obscure Icelandic comedies live on.

And without my father, Sal Bognanni, and his contagious love of cinema, I might not have fallen in love with movies the way I did. I think we saw forty matinees of *Return of the Jedi*, and you never complained. You showed me there was no better way to spend an afternoon. And Kathy Bognanni made sure I was always reading books, too. For that I am forever grateful. I think books and movies made up at least 50 percent of my childhood, and I have you two to thank for that.

Thank you, as always, to my family. Junita, who still says encouraging things no matter how many times I'm convinced that a book is no good. You believe in me more than I believe in me. Thank you to Roman who is now old enough to ask me, when I'm alternately laughing and frowning at the computer, "Are you writing, Dada?" And to Nico, who was just born, for sleeping sometimes, and smiling at me. I can't wait to take you to the movies.

Thank you to Namrata Tripathi for vastly improving this book. I wish you the best of luck on your new journey. It was a true privilege to work with you. Thank you to Jessica Dandino Garrison for bringing it all home with such insight and enthusiasm.

And to everyone else at Dial who seem to exist only to do nice things for my books.

Thanks to Kirby Kim, the man, the legend, for always going above and beyond, and to Brenna English-Loeb and the rest of the crew at Janklow & Nesbit. And thanks to Macalester College for letting me talk about stories all day with the best colleagues and students in the world.

Finally, since I have a tiny soapbox: go see independent films at your neighborhood movie theater! It will grow your soul and give you an excuse to eat a box of Sour Patch Kids.

PETER BOGNANNI is a graduate of the Iowa Writers' Workshop. His debut novel, *The House of Tomorrow*, won the LA Times award for first fiction and the ALA Alex Award and has been adapted into a feature film. His first book for teens, *Things I'm Seeing Without You*, was hailed as "required reading," "compelling," "original," and "hilarious" by critics and peers. Peter teaches creative writing at Macalester College in Saint Paul, Minnesota.